HONG KONG TALE-SPINNERS

A Collection of Tales and Ballads
Transcribed and Translated from
Story-Tellers in Hong Kong

HONG KONG TALE-SPINNERS

A Collection of Tales and Ballads
Transcribed and Translated from
Story-Tellers in Hong Kong

by

BERTHA HENSMAN, M.A., PH.D., D.PHIL.

and

MACK KWOK-PING, M.A.

with illustrations by

HSIEN CHUNG-Wu

THE CHINESE UNIVERSITY PRESS

The Chinese University Press
The Chinese University of Hong Kong
Shatin, New Territories, Hong Kong

© 1968 by The Chinese University Press
First Edition September, 1968
Second Edition June, 1977

International Standard Book Number 962-201-097-0

Printed in Hong Kong by Caslon Printers Ltd.

Dedication

to

Dr. Sidney D. Gamble

Life-Long Friend of China
and
The Chinese Christian Colleges
and
The Inspirer of this Book

ACKNOWLEDGEMENTS

The authors' thanks are due to people who have helped in the preparation of this book: to Miss Wu Chia-chun and the members of her family who spent long hours transcribing the recording of *The Dropped Fan* and supplying the Mandarin equivalents of the high proportion of expressions in that story peculiar to the Soochow dialect; to Mr. So Ping-shu who gave typing service; to Mr. Liang Lit-cheung who maintained contacts with the printers; to Mr. Brian C. Blomfield of Chung Chi College who proof-read the English manuscript for the printer; to Dr. Francis K. Pan, Director of Publications Office of The Chinese University of Hong Kong who, during the first busy month after assuming his new duties, undertook to guide the book through the final stages of publication; and above all to Dr. Sydney D. Gamble who first proposed the project and personally made funds available for the purchase of tapes and the costs of carrying out the preliminary stage of the project.

In the past four years Dr. Gamble followed with sustained interest and wise counsel each step of progress and each effort to overcome obstacles and set-backs. It is with profound sadness and deep regret that, in reply to an enquiry about the final stage of publication, we received the news that Dr. Gamble died on March 29th, 1968. It is fitting that this book should be dedicated to him without whose inspiration and encouragement the project would not have been undertaken.

B. H.

Chung Chi College   K. P. M.
Hong Kong
July, 1968

CONTENTS

ILLUSTRATIONS

FOREWORD

The Story-telling Tradition

The itinerant professional story-teller has, as far back in history as the Han Dynasty (206 B.C.—A.D. 220), been a familiar figure in China not only in the villages and remote hamlets but in the towns and cities as well. A Han Dynasty clay figurine of a seated story-teller of those far off days in North-west China provides clear evidence of the antiquity of the story-telling profession in Chinese tradition and of the animation with which the popular entertainer, even then, span his tale. The style of story-telling and some of the stories told have not changed basically through the long centuries between then and now.

In interior China up to 1949, on evening after evening as soon as dusk had deepened swiftly into darkness and the day's work on the farm, in the workshops, at the shop counter, or in the market place was done, the menfolk would gather in the neighbourhood teashop to sip tea, nibble melon seeds, peanuts and sweetmeats, while they talked over with associates and neighbours the market and farming prospects, local news, and national politics. The teashop served as an auditorium and provided a ready-assembled audience for the professional story-teller in much the same way that the modern city restaurant provides an evening floor-show, except that the teashop entertainment did not raise the cost of a bowl of tea.

In the villages of Szechuan and even in the capital, Chengtu, the street-level side of the teashop consisted of removable shutters which were closed only at night. Until 1949, throughout the long business hours, customers could literally step in from the street, passers-by could enter and leave freely or drop in for a long or a brief chat with friends and acquaintances who had stepped aside from the noisy eddying life of the street to drink tea in the comparatively quieter backwater of the teashop. There, at the cost of two or three cash, the proprietor provided at call an endless supply of boiling water to refill the initial bowl of jasmine tea or, with the addition of a brass bowl and soft towel, to enable the traveller to wash his dusty feet or sunburnt face. In the evening, when the teashop oil lamps gave more light than those of the dim street, the teashop customers provided a willing, captive audience for the professional story-teller.

Different Traditional Styles of Story-Telling

The style of story-telling was different in different parts of China.

Throughout the western part of Szechuan the professional story-teller would first pay the teashop proprietor an agreed fee. This done, he took his place each evening with a bowl of tea at a slightly raised table in a corner near the street and in full view of the customers. There, his face illuminated by the flickering naked flame of a floating wick of a vegetable oil lamp he would first clear his throat loudly, then take a long, noisy sip of tea, survey the teashop, and then give a sharp 'Clack' with his folding fan or with the wooden clappers which he held in his left hand. The customers would from then on divide their attention between their refreshments and their enjoyment of a dramatic recital in which the story-teller combined the arts of drama, opera, mime, sermon, story-telling and balladry. Passers-by, including women and children, would stand at the open shop-front listening to the tale. Unperturbed by occasional strident calls of "Lao Ban!

Tea here!", or 'Add boiling water here!', or "More peanuts, melon-seeds over here!" the tale-spinner would weave his tissue of a thousand and one nights' entertainment, punctuating his story at each critical juncture with a 'Clack' of his clappers or a swishing flourish of his fan ending in a sharp snapping sound as he closed it up.

This style of story telling is known as *p'ing hua* (平話) or plain style.

Another style, common in Soochow and throughout South China is the *p'ing-t'an* (評彈) style in which the story-teller enriches his tale with proverbs, rhymed couplets and folk songs such as the sententious advice which the Mountain God gives to the wicked young brother in *The Cock* in this volume. Such proverbial sayings were savoured as memorable 'jewels' which always gave a deeply appreciated literary flavour to a tale even in the vernacular.

A third, more elaborate style is the *t'an-tz'ŭ* (彈詞) style which originated and developed in and around Soochow and from there spread in less sophicated forms into the surrounding area of the Yangtse delta, northward to Peking and the Shantung peninsula, westward across North China, and north-westwards to the furthest boundaries of the country.

In the *t'an-tz'ŭ* style, the story-teller tells his tales to his own musical accompaniment which may be a three-stringed lute: (*san hsüen* 三絃), a seven stringed lute: (*ch'in* 琴), or a balloon-bellied guitar: (*p'i-pa* 琵琶), or a kind of zither: (*yang ch'in* 洋琴), or a small fiddle with a fixed bow of which the generic name, *hu* (胡), denotes its origin in the ancient home of the Han people in the north-west regions of modern China and beyond that, in Mongolia. The fiddle may be one of four strings (*hu ch'in* 胡琴), three strings (*san hsüen hu* 三弦胡), or two (*er hu* 二胡), but whatever the musical instrument the thin music subserves the story.

In the *t'an-tz'ŭ* tradition of story-telling, sometimes two narrators, traditionally two men, but in modern times sometimes a man and a woman or two women, cooperate in rendering the dialogue and the different episodes and shifts of emotion and emphasis in the tale they are telling, or in dramatizing their otherwise unannounced shifts back and forth between narrative, dialogue, soliloquy, and the story-teller's commentary in which he addresses the audience directly in explanatory asides.

In this collection of tales *The Dropped Fan*, although told by an individual story-teller, is in the *t'an-tz'ŭ* style and in the Soochow dialect, both of which characteristics posed particular difficulties to the transcriber and translator. On the one hand, the tale-spinner's sudden shifts from narration to soliloquy, from soliloquy to dialogue, from dialogue to chanted ditty, his interposed explanations, his modulations of voice all infuse into the oral tale an essential vitality which cannot be conveyed in cold print. On the other hand, the Soochow dialect is so different from Mandarin in vocabulary, idiom, and structure that before being able to embark upon translation the authors of this volume had to use an intermediary to help transpose into Mandarin their phonetic transcription of the tale as told in the Soochow dialect.

In all styles of story-telling the narrator remains seated and uses facial expressions and expressive gestures of hand, fan or handkerchief to give immediacy to his unfolding story. However, in the *t'an-tz'ŭ* style the expressions and gestures are often symbolic, bordering on mime, and the story-teller uses mimetic gestures more extensively than do those who narrate in the *p'ing hua* and *p'ing-t'an* styles.

Traditional Story-Telling — Then and Now

Prior to 1949, an evening teashop story-telling session would normally last one or even two hours during which the narrator would from time to time break off his story at a critical juncture, wipe his brow, sip his tea and pass a bowl around to collect money from his listeners. When the bowl was on its way back to him again he would carry on the story to the next major crisis and then once more exact the price of continuing. And so on for the full length of the evening's entertainment, during which he augmented the first takings of the evening by collecting several rounds of contributions from appreciative habitués and fresh contributions from late comers who had dropped in during a particular instalment of his tale.

The story-teller's livelihood was a precarious one in which he multiplied his occasions of earning by improvising inset episodes and by breaking off his tale-spinning evening at a juncture of high tension with a promise that he would go on from that point the following night. Some story-tellers would pad out a basic story so fully with invented episodes and improvised dialogue that they could carry it on in serial form for a month or more.

In making this collection, the narrators, who were paid by the hour, were advised to keep their inventiveness within reasonable limits but were also exhorted not to have so tight a rein on their inventiveness that they were not free to tell their story in their own way. The two stories, *The Beggar Defeats the Professional Boxer* and *The Dropped Fan* contain ample evidence of improvised padding and a lively use of popular appeal to a local audience in spite of the fact that, of necessity, they were recorded under conditions which entailed the absence of a responsive teashop audience to provide the natural interplay between the teller and the hearers of a tale in the oral tradition.

In China since 1949, professional story-tellers have been organized and led to use their traditional art in the service of their country. In each area they have formed a politically conscious artists' union and, under new incentives and purposefulness, have made great changes in the content and form of their repertory. They have discarded or transformed their old repertory of myths, legends, folk-tales, and high romance to give place to modern romances, chronicles, and epics which embody the heroism and achievements of Chinese people of to-day who, inspired by the leadership of the Chinese Communist Party, have served their country, even till death.

These modern tales, created for the audiences of a new age in China, are usually recitals of moderate length. The inordinately long, straggling romances of a more leisurely, less orderly pattern of society have been replaced by concise, self-contained episodes devised for the entertainment and explicit patriotic education of workers in factories, workshops, and communes in the interludes between work and study, and for the purposeful relaxation of the common people engaged upon mass-organized rural reconstruction projects.

Under new conditions of national life, professional story-tellers in China to-day have revolutionized and transformed their traditional art. But in the process they have ensured its survival by enlisting young artists of both sexes as apprentices who undergo, as of old, four or more years of arduous training under an acknowledged master of the art.

Since 1949, a few professional story-tellers of the old tradition have come to Hong Kong as refugees and, in the past eighteen years, have continued to earn a sufficient though precarious

livelihood. These story-tellers are now older men; they are
the last of a dying tradition in a new, industrial, urban society.
In village after village in the New Territories enquiries after a
story-teller or even for a traditional story draws a blank. It
seems that the transistor radio is superseding the teashop story-
teller. One or two of the older professionals are broadcasting
their tales in serial form and are now reaching a widely scattered
unseen audience in the resettlement areas of the city, the scattered
villages of the New Territories, and the remoter islands of the
Hong Kong waters. It is clear that the professional story-teller
who builds his tale and his style on the live interplay between
himself and the response of his audience is fast disappearing from
Hong Kong life. In our search we discovered only one young
story-teller who of necessity addressed herself to an unseen
audience. She was the blind girl from whose singing in *t'an-tz'ŭ*
style we recorded the two romantic ballads, *Ho Wai-kwan's Vigil*
and *The Lover to His Former Mistress*.

It seems therefore a matter of urgency that some of the
surviving traditional stories should be recorded before it is too
late. Besides, the few remaining story-tellers in Hong Kong
come from different parts of China and so use different dialects
and draw their stories from different sources and localities. So
the stories in themselves contain a wealth of materials for the
linguist, the literary historian, the sociologist and the philosopher-
historian whose main interest lies in the traditional ethics of
Chinese culture.

In addition to the professional story-tellers still functioning
in Hong Kong there are several less respectable, non-professional
ones who combine the roles of story-teller, quack doctor, furtune-
teller and medicine vendor. These story-tellers exploit to the
full, in the interests of their business, the live response of the

audience to their story as they tell it. They can be found in action after nightfall at all the seasonal fairs and popular festivals and, almost any evening, on the Hong Kong Harbour waterfront in one of the spaces left clear when the heavy lorries have ceased for the day their comings and goings to and from the Macao and Hunghom ferry terminals. There they stake out their stand with an open square of rough wooden benches within which they spread out on the ground their stock-in-trade of snakeskins, tiger bones, hartshorn, dragon's teeth, papers of dried herbs, bottles of liquid medicine, in short, traditional specifics for most of the diseases flesh is heir to. And central among their stock-in-trade, they usually spread out, anchored by stones at the four corners, a chart for phrenology, or fortune telling, or diagnosis, together with a basket of writhing, dangerous-looking snakes. The story-teller-herbalist then lights a pressure lamp and takes up his position, standing.

A crowd of grown men, who squat, perch or sit on the benches, soon collects. A bigger audience quickly gathers. Some members fill in the foreground of the enclosed space while others stand behind the benches peering between the heads of those who occupy the benches. With a few comings and goings in the rear, the audience remains for an hour or more listening to the vendor's performance and responding with ready laughter to his racy quips and venting loud guffaws at the points of broad humour in his tale which he tells with gusto in the low vernacular of the market place and waterfront.

The jostling crowds and the noises of the surrounding night market together with the ceaseless background roar and grind of passing traffic make it impossible to record these tales on the spot and so capture their essential savour and vitality. Moreover, these unprofessional story-tellers of the market place break off their yarns at fairly frequent intervals in order to indugle in equally animated sales-talk and to collect payments from those who purchase their medicines and advice.

The unprofessional nature of these story-tellers and the primarily commercial nature of the tales they tell rule their stories out of consideration for the purposes of this collection. Nevertheless, the popularity and continued presence of such men in the midst of a commercial city testifies to the strength of the story-telling tradition in Chinese culture in spite of the gradual disappearance of the professional story-teller from Hong Kong life.

In contrast to the non-professional spinner of popular yarns, the professional story-teller is a finished artist who has normally undergone an arduous three or four years' apprenticeship to his art. The stories in this small collection have been recorded, transcribed and translated from the story-telling of professional tellers of traditional tales who have, in the course of the last twenty years, come to Hong Kong from various parts of China. The range of dialects used in the various stories indicates the wide geographical area from which the dying tradition in Hong Kong has been drawn. Five of the thirteen stories were told in the Cantonese dialect, two in the Shanghai dialect, two in Mandarin, one in the Soochow dialect, one in the Chao Chow dialect of Kwangtung and one in the Hoi San dialect of the same province. The types of stories proved to be even more numerous than the dialects the tale-spinners use.

Types of Stories

The stories brought together in this volume were not selected on any pre-arranged plan. The collection began as an exploration of the field. Each tale was the choice of its narrator who told it in his own characteristic way. Yet in spite of the absence of design in selecting the stories we found that we had, by chance, assembled a wide variety of types of stories current in the oral tradition: a folk tale, a parable, a nature legend, a fable, a romance, a fairy tale, a popularized chronicle history, and one *wu hsia* or 'fighting knight-errant' story of earth-visiting immortals.

No professional story-teller lays claim to complete originality as far as his basic narratives are concerned. His originality lies in his artistry, in his powers of elaborating episodes, inventing and dramatizing dialogue, interpreting characters, in so bringing his skill into play that his tale becomes one which, in the words of Sir Philip Sidney, 'holdeth children from play and old men from the chimney corner'.

A few of the tales which the story-teller in the exercise of his art makes distinctively his own exist only in the oral tradition of his native district, but the majority of them have a literary source even though they may have reverted into the oral tradition before he takes them into his repertory. Some of the stories of magic, of ghosts, of supernatural happenings which he tells are of this kind. Even more certainly are the romances which he tells either as isolated episodes or in serial form. The commonest literary sources used in this way are the Sung Dynasty anthology of tales *Ta Sung Hsuan Ho Yi Shih* (大宋宣和遺事) first published in 1280, *The Water Margin* (水滸傳) first published in 1370, *The Romance of the Three Kingdoms* (三國志演義) which followed in 1585, and *The Dream of the Red Chamber* (紅樓夢) in 1763. In all cases episodes in these works were themselves based on stories current in a much older purely oral tradition or on an oral tradition whose distant antecedents lay in a literary tradition.

Chronicles and records of historical events interpreted in ethical terms and intermingled with myths, legends and tales of magic provide another source: such works as *The Book of History* (史記), 68 B.C. and *The Journey from the West* (西遊記), 1582.

Anecdotes of Taoist immortals or saints (仙), which are the Chinese equivalent of a cross between fairy tales and legends of the obscurer saints of the remoter period of Christianity in Europe, are another literary source. Of such a kind is the collection of *hsien* stories known as *Shou Shen Chi* (搜神記) first published in the year 320 A.D.

The cult of the *hsien* probably arose from the animistic religion of the country folk of China. It is first expounded and made relevant to religious philosophy in Taoist writings of the early years of the T'ang Dynasty (618-905 A.D.). For instance, Lao Tzŭ in the *Tao Teh Ching* (道德經), 480 B.C. summarises the powers of the person who, by self-control and ascetic disciplines of life and meditation, attains even while still a mortal, the super-natural powers of a *hsien:* 'he who has grasped the secret of *Tao* will be safe from the attack of buffalo or tiger . . . because he has no spot where death may enter'.

One of the oldest collections of *hsien* biographies is Liu Hsiang's (劉向) *Lieh Hsien Chuan* (烈仙傳), which was compiled during the Han Dynasty and circulated in manuscript until it was given wider circulation in a printed edition published between 1436 and 1449. The Chinese Encyclopedia, the *T'u Shu Chi Ch'eng* (圖書集成) published in 1726, contains over one thousand *hsien* biographies many of which, like those in Liu Hsiang's collection have merged long ago into popular variants or, in many cases, have been metamorphosed into tales of wonder and magic in the purely oral tradition.

The best known of the many *hsien* of Taoism are the group popularly known as the Eight Immortals. Chang Ko-lao (張果老), Chung Li-ch'uan (鍾離權), Tsao Kuo-k'ao (曹國舅),

Lu T''ung-pin (呂洞賓), Li T''ieh-kwai (李鐵拐), Han Hsiang-tse (韓湘子), Yen Tsai-ho (藍采和) and Ho Hsien-ku (何仙姑).

Some of the eight were historical persons of the T''ang Dynasty (618-905 A.D.) while some were added to the group in or after the thirteenth century. They employ supernatural and magical powers which enable them to control the forces of nature, command spirits, and appear and disappear at will in their beneficent or disciplinary relationships with men. One trio from among the eight has the strongest place of all in popular belief and story. It comprises Chang Kuo-lao, always depicted as a hermit, who carries prominently his long, magic-working castanets and, usually his monk's fish-shaped drum too; Lu T''ung-pin, also known as Lu Yen, always depicted as a long-gowned scholar, who carries at his back the huge two-edged sword which he wields with magical power in his battles for the cause of righteousness on behalf of the poor and oppressed; and Li T''ieh-kwai who was, historically, one of Lao Tzŭ's philosopher friends, and who is always represented as the lively beggar into whose body he was, by mischance, reincarnated. His symbols are an iron staff and the gourd inside which his disembodied spirit took refuge for a time before his reincarnation.

In the course of a thousand and more years these three have become characters in popular legends. They seem to be the prototypes of the 'Three Knights Errant of Szechuan' an episode of whose exploits is recorded here in the story, *The Beggar Defeats the Professional Boxer*. In Szechuanese folklore the original home of these three *hsien* is the Ch'in Ling Mountain Range of South Shensi Province. This north-west China mountain 'home of the gods' may indicate the route by which the tales of the legendary trio travelled from The Yellow River Valley to Szechuan, in the course of which journey, by oral transmission, the Taoist trio was transmuted into or identified with the heroes of Szechuan folklore.

Towards the end of the T'ang Dynasty the stories of the fighting exploits of various *hsien* stimulated the rise of another type of fiction known as *wu hsia* (武俠) which means *deeds of daring-do*, or *i hsia* (義俠) which may be translated as roughly equivalent to *Tales of Knight Errantry*, with the proviso that the aim of the Chinese knight errant was not, as in the *Tales of the Knights of the Round Table* in the European tradition, that of demonstrating chivalric virtues and rescuing fair damsels in distress, but that of concentrating on the fuller aim of Arthurian and Spenserian knights, the defeat of evil, the righting of wrongs, the just stripping down of vain pretentions and the punishment of deceit. In addition, the heroes of *wu hsia* tales have supernatural powers and a special method of fighting in which they demonstrate their mastery of the powers of the mind over those of the body.

As in the stories of Arthurian Knights, the *wu hsia* stories became modified and elaborated in the course of oral transmission so that in many cases their edifying purpose was submerged beneath the entertainment values of the tale itself.

Modern *wu hsia* stories are still a popular form of Chinese fiction. Each story is a self-contained episode in a series of exploits which are loosely held together, as in *The Beggar Defeats the Professional Boxer*, within the framework of a romantic tale in much the same way in which Chaucer's *Canterbury Tales* and Spenser's *Faerie Queene* are held together.

Another well-known literary source of tales, collected from the oral tradition of the seventeenth century, is P'u Sung-Ling's collection of ghost stories and folk tales of the supernatural which he completed in 1679. The stories circulated in manuscript for sixty years until they were published by P'u Sung-Ling's grandson in 1740.

P'u Sung-ling recorded in his biography that he had induced
people to tell him their stories which he wrote down at their
dictation and then subsequently dressed up in a literary style for
his collection of *Liao Chai Chi I* (聊齋志異), that is, *Strange Tales
of the Supernatural,* commonly referred to in Chinese as the
Liao Chai.

The two collectors and transcribers of the thirteen tales in
this present volume have allowed themselves no such liberty
but have restricted themselves to a faithful record of traditional
stories and have endeavoured to convey in the translation the
spirit of the original within strict bounds of fidelity to the words
as they were spoken.

Two years elapsed between recording *The Dropped Fan* and
completing the translation of it into English via a transcription
into phonetic symbols and a further transcription into Chinese
ideographs which entailed first, borrowing or inventing (*chieh
jung:* 借用) about 50% of the ideographs because there is no
written form for a great deal of spoken Soochow dialect and then
'translating' large passages of the story from Soochow dialect
into Mandarin.   Only then did we realize that the story was
incomplete, by which time Hong Kong was disrupted by the riots
and mob demonstrations of the summer of 1967.   As soon as
the situation returned to normal we tried to find the narrator—but
all our efforts to trace him have ended in failure.   Thus we are
compelled to leave our readers in the position of a teashop
audience when the story-teller breaks off his tale at a critical
juncture and leaves the listener impatient with curiosity to know
how the hero extracted himself from his predicament.   We cannot
satisfy the readers' desire to know how the story of *The Dropped
Fan* ends, but leave them expectant of more stories from the
repertory of the surviving Hong Kong tale spinners.

Hong Kong   B. H.
July, 1968   K. P. M.

PREFACE TO THE SECOND EDITION

The chief purpose of this second preface is the pleasant one of expressing my indebtedness and thanks to The Chinese University Press which has had the full responsibility of bringing out a new edition. The only changes made between this and the first edition consist of correction of misprints which escaped my vigilance when that edition was being printed.

Kirtlington,   B. H.
Oxford
1977

THE COCK

A very long time ago, on a mountain side, there lived an old woman. She had no children, and she gained a livelihood by ploughing the land and growing a few potatoes and turnips, so she led a hard and lonely life.

This old woman had reared a fat old hen which had become her sole companion. She loved it very much and fed it well. The old hen laid two eggs a day and the old woman used to exchange them for bran.

One day, the eggs that the old hen had laid could not be found. The old woman sought for them the whole of one afternoon, but in vain. Then she thought to herself, 'Perhaps the old hen has stopped laying eggs!' It did not matter very much if such was the case, only the old woman was worried, for what else could she depend on for her support in the days to come?

However, she noticed that the 'cackle-cackle' of the hen was somewhat different from the noise it used to make, and this fact surprised her a great deal. More than ten days passed in this way, and still she had not found the missing eggs.

One day, the old woman returned home from hoeing on the mountain slope to find that her old hen had completely disappeared. At first, overcome with grief, she wept bitter tears and blew her nose very hard. Next, she searched her little dwelling inside and out. Then, she combed the mountain-side searching for the hen. But after searching until evening, it had still not come home. She took the loss very much to heart and cried from night till morning and from morning till night. From then on, her life became poorer and lonelier than ever.

The Cock

The moon waxed and waned, and for a whole month the old woman yearned for her hen, until one night, she had a dream and dreamt that the Mountain God smiled at her and said, 'Dry your tears, Granny, your hen will come home soon! Then you will have many more hens to lay eggs for you; and I can promise you that you will then have two sons!'

The old woman was so overjoyed that she woke laughing from her dream. Before she had time to open her eyes, she could hear chickens chirrupping all over the floor of her little hut. She scrambled up in bed and saw her old hen flapping its wings and leading in more than twenty chickens to scratch for food on the floor of her room.

The old woman sprang down from her bed, snatched up the old hen, pressed it tightly to her bosom and would not let it go for a long time, while tears of joy rolled down her cheeks. The chickens, meanwhile, cluck-clucked noisily around her, and she bent and stroked each of them affectionately. Then she scattered some food on the floor for them, thinking as she did so, 'Upon my word! Where did all this good fortune come from?'

Now the truth of the matter was, that the old hen had laid its eggs in a mountain cave and had hatched out the chickens before bringing them home.

The chickens grew daily so that, in less than a month's time, the pullets began to lay eggs. But the two that were cocks grew even faster and bigger, with snowy white feathers, a bright red comb, orange-yellow legs and a long tail which glistened with silvery light. When they held out their chests and stretched forth their necks, they stood higher even than her table. When they strutted around the court-yard crowing, even the fierce mountain eagles were frightened and soared aloft and hid themselves high up among the clouds. Although the cocks could not lay eggs, the old woman felt a great joy and pride in just looking at them.

Gradually, sharp pointed spurs began to grow on the heels of the two cocks, and they fought fiercely, 'Clip-Clop', 'Clip-Clop', with their neck feathers erect. When they were not tearing out each other's white feathers they were tearing at each other's bright red comb. They fought countless times from morning till night. Once they fought so fiercely that they smashed all of the old woman's plates and dishes and even broke the cooking pot and filled the hut with clouds of dust. They even quarrelled during the night so that the old woman was robbed of her sleep.

From then on, she began gradually to be far less fond of them than she had been.

One day, very early in the morning before the old woman was up, when the magpies were chatter-chattering on the roof-top, all of a sudden, two strong healthy boys stepped out from the hen-roost. They ran straight into the old woman's room, fighting as they ran. They fought in this way until they stood before the old woman. Then, with one voice they called out affectionately, 'Mother! Mother!'

The old woman was dumbfounded. She did not know what to make of it all and dared not speak a word.

Later, when she remembered what the Mountain God had told her in the dream, she understood. Then she looked at the two boys with delight and could not help laughing heartily.

Then she gave them each a name. As a good omen, she called one 'Good Luck' and the other 'Good Fortune'.

The old woman was just going to turn round and cook them

something to eat when Good Luck and Good Fortune put up their fists and began to kick and fight again.

Then the old woman was alarmed and said to them angrily, 'Alas! You are brothers! Why do you persist in fighting like that?'

Good Luck and Good Fortune each pointed to himself and said:

'I want to be the elder brother!'

'I want to be the elder brother!'

The old woman read their minds, and so, after pondering for a little while, she said, 'Let's do this. Go to the mountain slope. There dig up some potatoes, and come back before this incense stick is burnt out. The one who can dig up most potatoes in that time will be accounted the elder brother.'

'Good! Good,' they promised with one voice.

So the old woman lit an incense stick and the two brothers were off to the mountain like two puffs of smoke.

Good Luck dug in real earnest and very soon filled a whole basket, but Good Fortune kept stopping after digging up each potato to see how much his brother had done. When he realized that he was far behind Good Luck, he scratched his head, and, unnoticed by anyone, held up his hands full of dust into the prevailing wind so that it blew straight towards Good Luck. Then, while Good Luck hurriedly covered his eyes with his hands, Good Fortune quietly tip-toed up, snatched his brother's basketful of potatoes and raced home like the wind.

As soon as the dust had settled, Good Luck saw that his basket of potatoes had disappeared and he hadn't the faintest idea where it had gone. Then it dawned upon him that Good Fortune must have played a dirty trick on him. But he also realized that there was still time to go before the incense stick would be burnt out. So he swallowed his anger and went on digging up potatoes at a great rate.

Now, while all this was going on, a magpie, perched upon a nearby tree top, had seen all that had happened. In fact, it had called out, 'Don't close your eyes! Don't close your eyes!' but Good Luck had not understood.

The bird was so worried about Good Luck that he had flown off to the mountain pass and had invited two anteaters to help him. They came, and they dug and they furrowed, dug and furrowed in the soil until all the potatoes lay on the surface.

In a trice, Good Luck gathered up two baskets full, balanced them at either end of his carrying pole, and raced back home with them raising a cloud of dust behind his heels as he ran.

The old woman, still holding the lighted stick of fragrant incense in her hand, stood waiting at the door. When she saw Good Luck carrying home such a big load of potatoes she was so happy that she burst out with a hearty laugh, 'Ha-ha-ha! There's no doubt whatever! Good Luck is the elder brother.'

As day after day passed by, Good Fortune nursed his grievance. Whenever the old woman was not present he would clench his fists and punch his brother. As the days went by the blows became more violent.

Then, one day, when the brothers went together to the mountain to cut firewood, they climbed a dangerous, high peak below which lay a deep pool whose dark, leafy-green waters instilled fear into the heart of any man who looked into their depth.

Good Fortune then pointed to an oak sapling and said to Good Luck, 'Elder brother, hard wood like that burns well. Let's cut down some of the branches for firewood for mother to use when she cooks our rice. My axe is too blunt for the job. You do it.'

Good Luck nodded his head in assent. Then he went to the edge of the precipice and raised his axe to chop off a branch. Then, when Good Fortune saw his elder brother totally engrossed in doing this, he gave him a shove and, with the push of one hand, sent him hurtling over the precipice. But he gave such a violent push that it carried him forward also with his brother and down with him into the depths of the pool below.

The two brothers sank and rose and swallowed a whole bellyful of water. In a very short time, that would have been the end of them but, at that very moment, the Mountain God intervened to save them. He built a path of stones out from the bottom of the pool and then called out, 'Good Fortune! Good Fortune! if you want to live you must, out of your own mouth, acknowledge your elder brother and take his hand in yours. And from now on you must stop attacking your elder brother. If you can bring yourself to do this then you can get out of the pool by walking along this stony path. But, if you refuse, you will surely die.'

Good Fortune at once promised to do as he was told. He called out to his elder brother by name and gave him his hand. And so the two of them walked out from the deep pool.

As they did so they heard a voice which said,

'When brothers live in harmony
Mountain boulders turn to jade.

When solitary man achieve community
The soil of earth transmutes to gold.
These words I give to you my sons;
Inscribe them indelibly upon your minds,
Engrave them deep upon your hearts,
Let nothing erode from your memory
This my counsel to you.'

With these words the Mountain God withdrew.

No sooner had the brothers emerged from the pool than Good Fortune totally ignored what he had heard. He turned to his elder brother and said, 'This place is really dangerous. Let's go somewhere else to cut our firewood.'

Good Luck, suspecting nothing, followed Good Fortune into a forest on the mountain side. They walked and walked, on and on. Good Luck had no idea for how long or into what part of the mountain they had ventured. They dripped with sweat and their stomachs gurgled and rumbled with hunger. But still Good Fortune did not stop.

When the sun began to set, Good Luck had walked until his head swam and his eyes were bleary, so he sat down on the ground to close his eyes and rest a while. When he opened his eyes again his younger brother was nowhere to be seen.

Good Luck was hungry too; and it grew so dark that he couldn't tell north from south, east from west. The night deepened. He wandered to and fro in the heart of the forest. He was completely lost. At last he died in a mountain cave and was turned into an echo.

As for Good Fortune, having led his elder brother into the wild and lonely mountain forest, and having made him lose his way, he hastened home alone. Nevertheless, he was afraid that Good Luck might follow him home; so he chose only the small by-paths to hurry along.

But his sense of guilt and his anxiety to reach home made him miss his footing—and he fell headlong into a pit which was lined on all four sides with thorn-bushes, so he could neither climb out nor move in any way. In desperation he called out for help. He lifted his head and shouted until his neck muscles were permanently stretched, but not the faintest reply came to his ears. He trembled from head to foot with fear and broke out in a cold sweat. Then, suddenly, from the top of the mountain, a voice full of irony called out, 'Good Fortune! Why don't you hurry home!'

Good Fortune stopped his struggles and looked upwards with his head well back. But all he could see was the Mountain God's face, looking at him from above the thick forest which clothed the mountain peaks. Good Fortune bowed his head in silence; he could do nothing else. Then the Mountain God, stroking his long beard, exhorted him earnestly,

'My child, you have a wicked heart. I ask you—can a single straw ever be made into a rope? or, can one man, using a carrying pole and one bucket, carry water from a well? A man who withdraws himself from others cannot help being useless. So I hereby restore you to your former shape. You will now become a cock again. Every day at sunrise you will have to go on searching for your elder brother, day after day, year in, year out, until you find him.'

Good Fortune then began to feel sorry for himself. The tears chased one another down his cheeks, but it was too late. He could say nothing. All he could do was to obey the Mountain God who thereupon changed him into a cockerel again, clad him in feathers and crowned him with a bright red comb. Then, 'Flap-flap', Good Fortune fluttered up out of the pit, and, stretching up his neck and calling 'Koh-Koh! Koh-Koh![1] Cock-a-doodle-doo!!' he went about calling for his elder brother and searching for him everywhere.

But, his elder brother had been changed into an echo and so could only echo the call from every side. And, to this very day, the cock has not found his elder brother. Yes; every day, year in, year out, the cock goes on searching for his elder brother and calls out loudly, even before daybreak, 'Koh-Koh! Koh-Koh! Cock-a-doodle-doo!!'

---

1.   In Chinese, Koh-Koh (哥哥) Elder Brother, is a word which has the same sound as the word used to denote the sound of a cock's crowing: (喌喌).

THE BLOCKHEAD

MANY years ago there lived in a village of Tsinan two men who had received their Hsiu-ts'ai degree[1]. One was surnamed Chang and the other Li. They were very close friends. Chang Hsiu-ts'ai was a landowner who possessed many herds of horses and cattle and whose rounded stacks of grain, large and small, were thatched and high-pointed like mountain peaks. In order to keep a firm check on his possessions, Chang spent the livelong day doing nothing but cast up his accounts as he busily flicked the beads of his abacus, 'Click-Clack, Click-Clack' from morning till night.

Now Chang Hsiu-ts'ai had a son to whom he gave the name Ts'ai-pao[2]. He so doted on this son that when the sun shone he was afraid the child would suffer a heat-stroke and when the cold winds blew he was afraid the boy would catch a chill. Therefore he kept the lad constantly indoors and forbade him even to go out without permission. Brought up in this way, when Ts'ai-pao was long past ten years of age, although he had read many, many books, he understood nothing, just like a wooden image in a temple.

Now it happened that Li Hsiu-ts'ai was the exact opposite of Chang Shou-ts'ai, for he had neither land nor paddy-fields and possessed no herds, either of horses or cattle. To support house and home he relied entirely upon his work as a teacher. He also had a son; and to this son he gave the name San-wên[3].

---

1. Hsiu-ts'ai: a title conferred upon those who had passed the first examination for official rank.
2. Ts'ai-pao: i.e. Precious Wealth.
3. San-wên: i.e. Benevolent and Alert.

The Blockhead

Every day, in addition to studying his reading and writing lessons, San-wên also helped his father and mother by doing odd jobs of all kinds about the house. And, by the time he was ten years old, he could write compositions, could supply the matching line of a couplet and could receive with proper courtesy the relatives and friends who called at the house.

One day, Chang Hsiu-ts'ai went to call on Li Hsiu-ts'ai to talk over some business matters. Arrived there, he saw a well-grown, well-fed donkey tied to a tree outside Li Hsiu-ts'ai's gate, so he admired the creature, saying aloud, 'What a fine, sleek animal! It's not often we meet with one like that!'

When San-wên knew that Chang Hsiu-ts'ai had arrived he hurried out, and, with a smile, said, 'That creature is nothing to speak of. It is hardly worth my Honourable Uncle's attention!'

While saying these words he ushered Chang Hsiu-ts'ai into the drawing room, which, although very simply furnished, was neat and tastefully arranged.

On entering the room, Chang Hsiu-ts'ai's attention was caught by a picture of the Goddess of Mercy painted by Wu Tao-tzŭ which was hanging in a prominent position on the far wall. He noticed that the artist, by the use of a few, simple brush-strokes, had produced an effect of vitality, and so, unable to restrain his delight and surprise, he asked San-wên, 'What painting is that?'

'That's an old T'ang Dynasty painting,' was San-wên's quick response.

Chang Hsiu-ts'ai then asked a further question: 'Is your father at home?'

San-wên immediately indicated the temple on the mountain side opposite the house, and said, 'He has just gone to the

White Cloud Temple for a game of chess with the old monk there.'

When Chang Hsiu-ts'ai saw that the boy had a quick mind and made intelligent answers he praised him heartily saying, 'What a bright lad you are! What a bright lad you are!'

When San-wên heard this praise, he at once replied with due humility, 'Thank you for your kind words, but your high praises embarrass me.'

Chang Hsiu-ts'ai waited for a while but Li Hsiu-ts'ai did not return, so he bade farewell and went home.

On his way home he thought to himself what a smart, courteous lad Li Hsiu-ts'ai's son was. And when he recollected the stupidity of his own son he found it extremely hard to bear. So, when he got home, he told his wife, in great detail, everything that had happened. Ts'ai-pao was in the room at the time and felt very disturbed when he heard his father speak in high praise of someone else, so he put his thumbs under his armpits and thrust out his chest and said, 'That's nothing! Get that fellow Li to come here. Don't think for a moment that I am incapable of uttering a few words like that!'

When Chang Hsiu-ts'ai heard his son speak in this manner he felt encouraged. So, in order to put his son's ability to the test, he tied a fat donkey to his own gate-post and borrowed an old painting from a friend's house and hung it in a prominent place in his guest hall. Then, when everything was ready, he sent special messengers to invite Li Hsiu-ts'ai to pay a visit.

When he saw that Li Hsiu-ts'ai was almost at the gate, he hastily hid himself in the room, behind the door, and there listened intently to overhear what Ts'ai-pao would say in reply to the visitor's questions.

The first thing Li Hsiu-ts'ai said was, 'Is your father at home?'

To which Ts'ai-pao proudly replied, 'That creature is nothing to speak of. He is hardly worth my Honorable Uncle's attention.'

'What's that you're saying!!,' replied Li Hsiu-ts'ai angrily.

'That's a T'ang Dynasty painting[4],' was the reply that came promptly to Ts'ai-pao's lips.

'Is your mother at home?' was Li Hsiu-ts'ai's next question, to which Ts'ai-pao still more quickly replied.

'She's just gone to the White Cloud Temple for a game of chess with the old monk there.'

When Li Hsiu-ts'ai heard Ts'ai-pao give such ludicrous ill-assorted answers to his questions, answers which were like the game of matching a horse's hooves with a cow's head, he realized that the boy was nothing more than a stupid blockhead and heaved a deep sigh and said, 'What a blockhead! What a blockhead!'

Ts'ai-pao thought that Li Hsiu-ts'ai was speaking to him again, so he hastily repeated San-wên's last sentence, 'Thank you for your kind words, but your high praises embarrass me!'

Meanwhile, Chang Hsiu-ts'ai was so overcome with confusion and shame that he felt unable to emerge from his hiding place behind the door.

---

4. A play on words. 話 *words* and 畫 *painting* have the same pronunciation in Chinese: both are pronounced *hua*.

聚寶盆

一九六八年三夏中吾繪

The Magic Treasure Pot

THE MAGIC TREASURE POT

ONCE upon a time, there lived a boy who was called Little Wong. He and his mother were very poor and they worked for a wealthy landlord.

Little Wong's mother did sewing and washing for the landlord and fed his pigs and ducks, while Little Wong, day after day, went out onto the hillsides to cut fresh grass to feed the landlord's horse.

Day after day he cut grass, and so, day after day, there was less and less grass on the hillsides for him to cut. Then the day came when Little Wong had cut all the grass he could find, both on the near side of the hills and on the far side, and by early afternoon, all he had for his trouble was one small truss of grass. He was very worried and very afraid, because the landlord expected him to bring back, every day, a full load of grass on each end of his carrying-pole. But on this day, by early afternoon, all he had to show was one small truss of grass. So he thought to himself, 'What shall I do? If I carry back only this much grass, how can I avoid being beaten by my master?'

So he dared not return home. Instead, he went further afield to some distant mountain slopes.

He walked and walked, until he saw, on a distant mountain slope, a meadow of lush green grass rippling in the breeze. He walked towards it and, when he reached the place, rejoiced to see such tall, juicy grass. With great excitement, he began to cut, and, in a trice, he had cut a full load of it. But, as he cut and cut, he wondered, 'How can this be? As fast as I cut this grass, more springs up in its place. It's beyond me!'

He neither turned around nor moved from the place where he first began to cut, and yet, in less than no time, he had cut several trusses of grass. He didn't have to hurry. He just cut two or three more trusses and he had enough to make a full load for carrying home. Stroke by stroke he cut in a leisurely fashion, and so had time to glance side-ways and noticed that the grass sprouted up tall again as swiftly as a dart from a blow-pipe.

This was very strange and very exciting. When he had cut a full carrying-load of grass, it was not yet sunset, so he rested a while before he felt it was time to go home. Then he tied up his trusses of grass into a load for each end of his carrying-pole. This done, he took a large pebble and used it to mark the place where he had been cutting. Then he balanced the load on either end of his shoulder-pole and set off for home.

From then onwards, day after day, Little Wong went back to the same place, and, day after day, he cut a full load of grass and, before noon, was off home again.

Now the landlord became very surprised at this and asked, 'Little Wong, how does it come about that you can cut a load of grass and can still be back here again so soon? Where did you cut the grass?'

Little Wong replied, 'For some days now, I've found a place where the grass grows thick, and so I've managed to cut a load of it very quickly.'

With a sinister smile the landlord replied, 'Ha! That's fine! From tomorrow onwards, you can cut and bring an extra load, each day, for my chestnut horse.'

There was no way out of it. Little Wong had to go and cut grass as the landlord had ordered him.

Again he was amazed at how the grass sprouted up again as fast as he cut it, so he told his mother what was happening.

His mother was also amazed and said, 'My son, take me along with you tomorrow.'

The next day, Little Wong was soon back with his first load of grass. He put the grass in the stable and then secretly took his mother along with him on the second trip. He led his mother along to the place on the mountain side where he had been cutting grass every day. Then he took out his sickle and cut grass while his mother first stood staring and staring, astounded by what she saw. Then she snatched the sickle from her son's hand and began to cut grass herself. The same thing happened as when her son was cutting—as fast as she cut a swath of grass, grass sprouted up again in its place, as tall as it was before. On seeing this, Little Wong's mother was more taken aback than ever, and murmured to her son, 'This is amazing! There must be something magical about this place—otherwise, how could such a thing as this be happening!'

Then mother and son together seized the sickle and began digging. They dug, and dug, and, finally, they dug up a small, earthenware bowl.

Little Wong was very disappointed and exclaimed, 'We've worked for half a day and we've tired ourselves out, and all we've dug up is this child's plaything. What use is it?'

But his mother said, 'I don't see that it's of much use, but, after we've had all the trouble of digging for it, let's at least take it home and use it as a feeding trough for the ducks.'

So Little Wong's mother carried the earthenware bowl home to the landlord's house and used it as a feeding trough for the ducks. She put food into it for the ducks, and the whole flock ate their fill, but the food in the bowl not only didn't grow less, it overflowed onto the ground.

Now Little Wong's mother didn't notice this, but, one day, the landlord did, and he berated and scolded her: 'Can't you pay more attention to your job! You don't even know how to feed ducks! The duck-feed is spilling all over the place, you good-for-nothing creature!'

When Little Wong's mother heard the landlord speak to her in this way she sulkily picked up the earthenware trough, cleaned it out, and put it away.

One day some time later, when she was busy sewing, she accidentally dropped a broken end of thread into it, and, before her very eyes, the broken end of thread grew and grew until it filled the bowl and, in next to no time, it had covered the whole k'ang.

Little Wong's mother was amazed to see this, and was afraid that somebody else might see what was happening, so she quickly snatched the bowl up. At once the thread stopped overflowing onto the k'ang.

That evening she told her son all about it.

'This is something stupendous! How could it come about that an end of thread, thrown away into this earthenware bowl, could, in next to no time, grow into a pot-full of thread, and even overflow until it covered the k'ang. It's more than likely that this earthenware bowl is what folks might call a magic treasure-pot.'

As she said this, she reached into the triangular cloth pocket, which her son wore close to his body at the front of his belt, and took out several copper coins, and threw them into the earthenware bowl. And before her very eyes, the copper coins multiplied and,

in a trice, it was full.   She stared wide-eyed, while it overflowed
with coins until, with a tinkling sound, they overflowed to every
corner of the k'ang.

Mother and son were overjoyed to see this, and then the
mother said, 'My word!   Here's a lot of money indeed!   We've
been poor long enough.   We shall be well off now!'

So the mother and son drew their last wages from the landlord
and, from that day on, refused to work for him any more.   But
they still went on living in the same old straw hovel.   As soon
as they had spent their money, they did the same as before and,
whenever they cast a few copper coins into the earthenware bowl,
it overflowed with copper coins, and when they cast silver coins
into it, it overflowed with silver coins.   Mother and son depended
upon this magic treasure-pot as their source of income, and so
were very well off.

Meanwhile Little Wong still went up into the hills every
day to cut and collect firewood.   He had a load for sale every
day in addition to the wood they needed for their cooking and
so, every day, he brought back with him from the market something
special for his mother to eat.   And from that time on, the clothes
of mother and son were always neat and clean.

The villagers noticed the change that had taken place and
whispered among themselves, 'Mrs. Wong and her son have given
up working for their landlord.   Neither of them does any work.
All they've got to depend on is what Little Wong earns by cutting
and collecting firewood and selling it.   Where do they get all
the money they spend?'

There's no way of knowing how people got to know about
Little Wong's magic treasure-pot, but the news did get about,
and finally, it reached the landlord's ears.

Now, whenever that landlord smelt money, he went hot-foot

after it. So he immediately sent messengers to Little Wong's
home to claim the ducks' earthen feeding trough as his property;
and on this false claim, they carried it away.

When the landlord got the earthenware bowl into his possession
he cast a silver ingot into it, and, immediately, the bowl overflowed
with silver ingots. He was overjoyed and invited his aged father
to come and see the magic treasure-pot.

When his father entered the house, he clapped his hands
at seeing the place flooded with silver ingots. But the old
man had reached a very ripe old age, so he didn't see clearly
where he was going, and he fell with a clinking 'Ding-ding-dang'
among the ingots and landed on the earthen treasure-pot. And,
as the bowl broke into pieces, every last ingot on the floor
disappeared.

FAN KIANG-SHAN AND THE TIGERS

SUMMER had come and the wild peach trees on the hills were laden with peaches, when, one day, Fan Kiang-shan went up the hill to break ground for a new field and there he saw, growing at the side of a pot-hole, a tree laden with ripe peaches. He wanted some to eat, so he put down his spade and climbed the tree.

Just at that moment a family of tiger-cubs appeared on the scene. They surrounded the peach-tree, and stared at Fan Kiang-shan. At this Fan was somewhat scared for he wondered whether or not they intended to eat him. However, he managed to keep calm in spite of his fear, and, with a smile addressed the cubs, 'Would you like to have some of these peaches to eat?'

The cubs all smiled and nodded their heads, so Fan Kiang-shan knitted his eyebrows thoughtfully and said, 'I would like to throw some down to you but I'm afraid that when they hit the ground they will bounce into the pot-hole. You'd all better go and fetch either a blanket or a straw sleeping mat.'

The cubs nodded their heads and hurried away.

While they were away Fan Kiang-shan thought at first he would jump down from the tree and run away but, on second thoughts, he said to himself, 'Tigers are dangerous creatures. Why shouldn't I take this opportunity of getting rid of them, all at one go?' So he didn't run away.

In less time than it takes to have two puffs at a tobacco pipe, the cubs came panting back dragging with them a big straw sleeping-mat.

Fan Kiang Shan and the Tigers

Fan Kiang-shan asked them to place the mat over the mouth of the pot-hole. Then he threw down the peaches, one at a time, onto the mat.

The cubs couldn't wait until Fan Kiang-shan had finished throwing down the peaches. Each one of them, struggling to be first and afraid to be last, jumped onto the mat to devour the peaches. Then suddenly, 'Wah!!' the mat gave way under them and cubs and peaches together all tumbled into the pot-hole.

When the mother tigress learned about this she rushed to where Fan Kiang-shan was and besought him to haul her cubs up to safety. But Fan Kiang-shan only smiled and said, 'I know! Let's throw stones into the pot-hole until the hole is filled up, and then the cubs can climb out by themselves.'

The tigress believed what he said and quickly hurled stones into the pot-hole so that the hole would be filled up in the shortest possible time.

By the time the pot-hole was filled up, all the little tigers had been stoned to death. They were buried so deep beneath the stones that they could never have got out even if they had survived.

The tigress wailed for some time. Then she glared fiercely and wanted to devour Fan Kiang-shan. So Fan Kiang-shan said to her, 'Don't be in too much of a hurry. There's a much more suitable place than this where you can eat me up. Let's go down to it—it's at the bottom of the cliff where no one will see you do it.'

The tigress agreed to this proposition and so followed him down the cliff to a big rock at the bottom.

This cliff was so very steep-sided that if you looked up from the bottom you could see only the clouds floating by up above while you would feel that the boulders were going to crash down upon you, for even the bushes and plants looked as if they were being forced downwards. And when a gust of wind blew through the place, it made such a deep moaning sound in the gully that you felt as if the cliff was going to topple down on your head. So Fan Kiang-shan exclaimed, 'This won't do! This won't do! The cliff is going to fall down and crush us to death!'

At these words the tigress took fright and appealed to Fan Kiang-shan to get them out of the dangerous situation.

He thought for a second and then said, 'Quick! Lift up your front paws and help to prop up the cliff while I go and cut down a tree to buttress it so that it doesn't come crashing down upon us.'

The tigress could only do what he said. She thereupon lifted her front paws to prop up the cliff with all her strength until her face was livid with the effort.

Fan Kiang-shan nodded his head at her with approval and, just before he went off, exhorted her, 'Whatever you do, don't relax the pressure, otherwise the whole cliff will come rattling down and will crush you to death. Wait till I get back before you relax your pressure. Now don't forget!'

The tigress was so impressed by what Fan Kiang-shan said that she dared not relax her position even for a moment. She waited and waited. She waited three whole days and nights, but not a sign did she see of Fan Kiang-shan's return. She held on until her will-power and strength came to an end and then she dropped down almost dead from exhaustion.

When the father of the cubs found out what had happened, he determined to get his revenge for what had happened to his wife and so came panting in hot haste after Fan Kiang-shan.

Fan Kiang-shan was cutting firewood in a lonely part of the mountains when he saw the tiger coming. He knew at once what the tiger had come for, so, taking out his cowhorn, he said to him, 'Let me just blow this horn for you and let the music help you to calm down, and then there'll still be plenty of time for you to eat me up!'

But the tiger didn't bother to reply. He was only intent on eating up Fan Kiang-shan at once. So Fan Kiang-shan began to get really worried and took up his horn and blew a blast upon it. The tiger liked the sound of the horn so very much indeed that he gave Fan Kiang-shan a chance to finish the tune before he settled down to the job of eating him up.

The more the tiger listened to the tune, the more he liked it. He closed his eyes, beat time with his head, waved his tail in time with the melody and, finally, began to sing, until he was entranced and completely lost in the music. Then suddenly, someone fired a gun, the tiger's skull was smashed into fragments and, at the very moment of the shot, he dropped down dead.

Now this is what had happened. When the people living on that mountainside heard Fan Kiang-shan blowing his horn, they knew that he had met a tiger. So they at once took up their guns, shouldered their spears and came in a body to the rescue. But when they arrived and saw the tiger dancing in front of Fan Kiang-shan and swaying as if under the influence of drugs, they were amazed and at the same time so amused that they couldn't help smiling. Then, with one shot, they killed the tiger.

From that time onwards, all tigers, large and small, hated Fan Kiang-shan and were on the look-out for a chance to kill and eat him.

Then, one day, when Fan Kiang-shan was ploughing his field, he suddenly found himself surrounded by a dozen or more tigers.

First of all, the old tiger, who was the leader of the pack, sprang upon Fan Kiang-shan's ox and killed it at the first bite, and then asked him, 'Why have you always set yourself against us? Today, it's our turn to give you some rough treatment.'

When Fan Kiang-shan looked at his dead ox, he felt heart-broken and thought within himself, 'They have killed my ox. I will remain their enemy till the last ditch.'

But he couldn't say this openly, so he held his peace. Inwardly he was contemplating how to deal with those tigers, but in actuality, he realized that here and now he was in a very dangerous predicament.

Then the old tiger turned to him and said, 'Fan Kiang-shan, why do you have nothing to say for yourself today? You generally have quite a lot to say. You're so clever at deluding others you probably possess a copy of the *Book of Lies*.'

When Fan Kiang-shan heard the tiger ask this he quickly thought up a new scheme, and so answered at once, 'I do possess a copy of the *Book of Lies*. I inherited it from my ancestors. If you could study that book you too would know all about how to delude others and no man would be able to catch and kill you.'

When the tiger heard these words he secretly rejoiced, and thought, 'Let's first get our hands on that *Book of Lies*, and, that done, we'll eat him up. That's the idea!'

Then he spoke his thoughts aloud and said, 'If you surrender that *Book of Lies* to us, we won't eat you.'

Fan Kiang-shan nodded his head in agreement and said, 'I'll go and fetch it, but it's an unusually queer book. Anyone who wants to read it must first bind himself hand and foot before he can even see it. If he doesn't do that, the *Book of Lies* will fly away even from before his eyes.'

The tigers thought that there might be a trick in this and

so were unwilling to be bound hand and foot.   So Fan Kiang-shan
said to them, 'Very well!   Eat me then!   But if you do, you will
never be able to get hold of that *Book of Lies*, and, sooner or later,
men will surely catch and kill you.'

Now the tiger very much wanted to get possession of that
intriguing *Book of Lies*.   So he thought to himself, 'A dozen or
more tigers are more than a match for one man.   The best thing
to do is to let him come and tie us up.'

So Fan Kiang-shan went and fetched a dozen or more lengths
of very strong rope and, one by one, he trussed up those tigers,
dead tight.   Then, when he had tied up the last of them, with
one sweep of his arm he picked up from the earth the shaft of his
plough-share and, using it with all his might and main, struck
each one of them on the head, saying at every blow, 'This is the
Book of Lies.'

And at every blow the tigers moaned aloud, for they realized
that they had once again fallen into his trap.   But they were tied
up so tightly, legs and paws, that they had no way of getting free.
And by the evening, Fan Kiang-shan had beaten every one of the
dozen or more tigers to death.

From that day onwards, Fan Kiang-shan hated tigers more
than ever.   He thought up many other schemes whereby he killed
more and more tigers until at last there was only that one mother
tigress left alive on the whole mountain-side.

Now this tigress had fled from the mountain and had
nowhere to go.   Finally she thought of one last way out of
her difficulties: that was, to go to the capital and take out a
summons against Fan Kiang-shan.   So she hurried off to the
capital and, somehow or other, managed to get into the Imperial
City[1].   There the Emperor asked her what she had come for.

---

1.   The Imperial City is the walled city of imperial buildings within the
     capital.

With tears streaming down her face she pleaded, 'Among the Miao tribespeople of West Hunan there is a fellow named Fan Kiang-shan who has killed off practically all of us tigers, until I am the only one left. I beseech Your Majesty to give judgement in my favour.'

The Emperor saw that she was in a pitiable state and so had compassion on her and said, 'I grant you to have nine cubs in one litter. In this way, as the years go by, and before many years are past, your children and grand-children and their children will become more and more numerous.'

When the tigress received the emperor's verdict, she was filled with joy, and set out again for West Hunan. And all the way home, she kept on repeating to herself, 'Nine cubs to every litter!'

But, when she was halfway home, she came face to face with Fan Kiang-shan, and she was so scared that every word the emperor had spoken to her was driven out of her head. All she was capable of doing was to beg Fan Kiang-shan to spare her life and to tell him that the emperor had promised her that she would bear many more cubs. But she couldn't remember how many cubs he had said she would bear in one litter. So Fan Kiang-shan prompted her and said, 'Oh, I know that. The emperor promised you that you would bear one cub every nine years.'

The tigress believed what Fan Kiang-shan said, and trotted off to her mountain home, where, nine years later, she gave birth to one solitary cub.

That is why, today, there are so very few tigers in the Western part of Hunan Province.

THE HAIR ROPE BRIDGE

PEOPLE say that Chu Yün[1] Mountain on the south bank of the Poyang River and the Hsien Hua[2] Mountain on the north bank were originally one single mountain and that one of the Immortals, by using his magic wand, split the mountain and caused a big river to flow between the two halves. There is a story behind this legend, the story of the Hair Rope Bridge.

Many years ago, there lived at the foot of this mountain a young man named Chu Yün. He was not married, and he was both hard-working and kind-hearted. Every day he arose before daylight, lit his fire, cooked his rice, took up his wood-cutter's knife, tied up his leaf-wrapped balls of cooked rice into his lunch-cloth and set off for the mountain.

By the time be had climbed a considerable way up the mountainside, the sun had only just begun to peep. Then he chopped and chopped underbrush until, by noon, he had cut enough firewood to make a load for each end of his carrying pole, and so could sit down to relax for a while before he opened up his lunch-cloth and ate his rice-balls. Then he scooped up some clear, spring water and drank it from his cupped hands. Next, he took his flute out from his waistband and 'Tweedle-dee, tweedle-dee', he began to play.

Now Chu Yün knew kow to play the flute so well that the melody hovered in the air, the white clouds floating overhead stopped to listen, the leaves of the trees ceased their rustling, the

---

1. Lit. i.e. 'Purple Cloud'.
2. Lit. i.e. 'Fairy Flower'.

The Hair Rope Bridge

breezes were silent, the birds stopped singing, and the goats and wild rabbits sat still to hear.

When he had played his flute for a short while, he balanced his load, shouldered his carrying pole, and went down the mountainside where he sold his load of firewood, bought a supply of rice, and then went back to the solitude of his home.

Year after year, things went on in this way. Day after day, before daylight, he went up the mountain to cut firewood and there waited for the dawn. Then there came a day when he went up the mountain and, as usual, by noon, had cut a load of firewood, but, just as he was sitting down to eat his rice-balls, what a surprise! On opening his lunch-cloth, the rice was quite different from usual. It was piping hot and fragrant steam rose from it. Was it because of the hot weather? No; it was now just after mid-Autumn, so the weather was already turning cold.

Although very suspicious of what he found, he ate the rice. Then, when he had eaten, he stretched his hand behind him to take down his patched and mended jacket which he had hung on a low pine-branch. 'Hello!' The darns and patches were gone; the jacket was like a new one.

Had somebody else left it there? But he knew that nobody had passed that way all day. Could there be any doubt that it was his?—It was clearly the one which he had worn for the past ten years, the one he had patched and mended for the past ten years. He could recognize the very patches that his mother had sewn on it many years before, except that now the darns and the edges of the patches were absolutely smooth, as if it were a new garment.

By this time the hour was late, so with no more ado Chu Yün put the jacket on and went down the mountain, home.

The next day, the day after that, and the day after that, Chu Yün went up the mountain to cut firewood, and day after day the same extraordinary things happened. His cold rice-balls turned into fragrant, steaming-hot rice and if his jacket happened to be torn, he found it mended. If it was dirty, he found it spotlessly clean.

For a long time, Chu Yün wanted to get to the bottom of the mystery. Who could it be who took his bundle of rice-balls every day and made them hot while he wasn't looking? Who could it be who took his torn and dirty clothing and mended and cleaned it while his back was turned? So, one day, in order to find out, he put his lunch bundle and his jacket on a stone at the foot of a pine tree not far from where he was cutting wood and at every other stroke he glanced towards the pine tree. Time passed by and still nothing happened either to his lunch bundle or his jacket which still lay at the foot of the pine tree.

'Why is this so?' he wondered and, as he thought, he lifted his eyes towards the heavens. And, in that moment, his food-bundle and his jacket disappeared! He quickly glanced around him in all directions, but nothing unusual could be seen, except in the far distance, he espied two white kids making for the mountain top. One of them was carrying off his food bundle in its mouth and the other his jacket, so he threw down his big knife and ran after them.

The two kids raced on ahead with leaps and bounds with Chu Yün following cautiously after them. They crossed mountain slopes, they sped along the edges of high cliffs, and then, in the twinkling of an eye Chu Yün lost sight of them and found himself in a wonderful valley where grew thick clumps of leafy trees and, all around, grew strange and beautiful flowers and plants.

While he was walking about in this valley, the smell of fragrant rice came wafted to his nostrils. He stood still, uncertain where the smell was coming from, and then realized that it was coming from a cave. So he went over to the cave.

When he first stepped inside the cave, it was pitch dark, but, on going a little further in, he suddenly found himself in a brightly lit room with gleaming windows, and with polished chairs and the rest of the furniture neatly and tastefully arranged.

The two kids were frisking and playing about in the room while new-cut firewood sizzled and crackled under a pot which stood upon the mud-built stove, and, from the pot, the fragrant steam of rice just cooking billowed out into the room. Then a young woman, holding his jacket in her left hand and a needle of thread in her right, stepped forward to welcome him.

Chu Yün was surprised indeed to see this beautiful young woman caught in the act of mending his coat. As for the young woman, when she saw Chu Yün standing before her, she cast her eyes down in bashfulness while Chu Yün stood uncertain how to behave. So they both stood in great embarrassment, both of them blushing up to the ears. Then, after standing thus, tongue-tied, they gazed into each other's eyes.

Now, when a kind-hearted, hard-working young bachelor meets a beautiful, tenderhearted young lady, it normally doesn't take them long to fall in love and, before long, to agree to marry one another. And so it was.

Now who was this young woman? She was Hsien Hua, the daughter of the God of Longevity who dwelt in Heaven. But she chose to dwell below, on earth, on this mountain-side, and her father came to visit her once every four or five years. She had been looking out day after day from this cave, where she passed her days spinning and weaving, and, day after day, before the sun was up, she had seen Chu Yün coming up the mountain to cut firewood. She had listened to him playing his flute and had gradually fallen in love with him. She had felt sorry for him having to eat cold rice-balls day after day and having no one at home to wash and mend his torn and dirty clothes and so, every day, she had been steaming his rice-balls and washing and mending his clothes for him. She had felt that it was not proper for her to go out to where he was working, so she had been sending the two kids to take up his food and clothes and bring them back to her in their mouths.

Now when Chu Yün and Hsien Hua got married they set up home together in the cave. Soon the trees burst forth in new, green leaves. Then the leaves fell. Then a second Springtime came round, and a third. And in this way, several years passed by.

As the years passed, they had five children, all of them sturdy and good-looking.

In the daytime, Chu Yün went onto the mountainside to cut firewood and to clear patches of ground where he planted various crops. Meanwhile, Hsien Hua busied herself in the cave, spinning and weaving while the children played happily around her. Then, in the evening, the whole family gathered together. In this way they lived in happiness and contentment.

Then there came a day when Chu Yün felt a longing to revisit his old home at the foot of the mountain. So, having gained Hsien Hua's consent, he set off down the mountain taking the five children with him.

It so happened that the God of Longevity chose this very day to come down to Earth to visit his daughter Hsien Hua.

On entering the cave, he noticed there was something different about it. He wondered, and then asked Hsien Hua what had been going on. Hsien Hua was a straightforward young woman and so she told him about all the changes that had taken place since his last visit.

When he heard what she had to say he was very angry. To think that the daughter of an Immortal should marry a human being!

Simmering with anger at being powerless to do anything about it, he sped to the top of the mountain peak, lifted his magic sword, smote the air towards the foot of the mountain and cleft the mountain asunder, straight, from top to bottom. At once, a deep rumbling sound resounded through the skies as if the whole earth were falling apart. The heavens were blotted out with cloud and mist and, when the clouds and mists cleared away, you could see that the mountain had been, as it were, cloven in two, split asunder, with a big river flowing between the two halves. The currents of the river were so turbulent that their seething white crests rose almost to the sky.

And from that day to this, Hsien Hua and Chu Yün have been two separate mountains.

Now, when Chu Yün reached where his old home was, wanting to show it to his children, not a sign of it could he find. The house had collapsed and crumbled into dust. So he retraced his steps to take the children home again. But he little thought that he would find the path cut off by a big river more than a hundred yards wide. When he saw this, he wept aloud, he couldn't help it, for he thought he would never see Hsien Hua again.

The children also wept, and wailed, and called upon their mother, but to no avail. Chu Yün was not a bird. He had no wings with which to fly across the deep river. Chu Yün was not a fish. He had no fins with which to swim across the wide waters.

All he could do was, with a heavy heart, to lead his children to search for a resting place where they could make a new home on the mountain side.

After this, by day he cut firewood and cleared patches of ground which he tilled to grow their food. When evening came he sat on the mountain peak and played his flute. And the wave-like melody wafted across the river and reached the topmost peak on the other side, where, in the silence of the night, Hsien Hua lay longing for Chu Yün. In this way, their hearts' longings flowed to each other across the gap between.

Meanwhile, day after day, Hsien Hua stood on the topmost mountain peak, longing for Chu Yün and yearning for him and for her children, her heart burdened with sorrow for their plight. She blamed her father for his heartless cruelty. But what could she do about it? What could she do so that her family would be brought together again?

Her first thought was that she might build a long, long bridge across the river. But what materials could she find to build a bridge with? She thought and thought, and then, suddenly, she noticed her own long hair which lay thickly about her shoulders like a cape. Ha! she might braid her long hair into a plait and use that as a bridge.

So she spent her days spinning and weaving, but, in the evenings, to the accompaniment of Chu Yün's flute, and with tears streaming down her face, she plaited her own hair. Evening after evening, night after night, she plaited and plaited, her tears mingling with her braided hair. She plaited away in this manner for three years and six months until she had made one long sleek, gleaming plait, exceedingly strong.

But now, how could she cast the end of the plait across the

river so that it would anchor on the other side?   She did not know how to solve this problem.   And when she thought of her wasted three and a half years of time and effort, she wept bitterly once more.

She wept and wept and wept aloud until the very stars of heaven hid themselves behind the clouds, the birds left their forest homes, and even the Ancient Spider who dwells in a cranny of the cliff was moved to pity her.

Now the Ancient Spider was determined to help and succour the unfortunate pair, so he span out from his mouth a long, long silken cobweb thread.   Then a gust of wind blew it across the river, where it caught on the branch of a pine tree which was growing on the top of the opposite cliff.   Next, the Ancient Spider, holding one end of the plait in his front legs, crawled slowly along the cobweb thread, and so across the river.

That day, Chu Yün was making a new clearing for cultivation when he looked up and saw the spider dragging the long plait along the cobweb thread.   He at once realized what it all meant.   When the Ancient Spider had landed safely, Chu Yün immediately anchored the end of the plait to the pine tree.   Then, one by one, the children joyfully stepped upon the plait of their mother's hair which she had used to make a bridge, and so, one by one, they crossed over the river.

Although the currents below surged along, and although the bridge was very narrow and swung in the air at every step, the love their mother had for them gave the children courage, so that, one by one, all five got safely across.

Then Chu Yün stepped upon the soft and swinging bridge and he too got safely across.   And so husband and wife and children were reunited to make their home together once more.

Their strong, pure love, their courage and their endurance so moved the heart of the God of Longevity that he decided not to interfere with them any more. And so, they passed the rest of their lives in great happiness, Chu Yün cutting wood and tilling the soil, Hsien Hua spinning and weaving.

From that day to this women have grown their hair long and have braided it into long plaits, and from that day to this, the two tall mountains on either side of the Poyang River have been called Chu Yün Mountain and Hsien Hua Mountain.

THE SNAKE WILL SWALLOW THE ELEPHANT [1]
OR
THE OVER-REACHER

THERE once lived a man named Wong San who went up into the mountains every day to cut brushwood for fuel which he sold and then used the money to support himself and his mother.

Every morning, before he set out for the mountain, his mother gave him a big, flat, round millet cake to take with him for his lunch.

One day, Wong San had cut brushwood all morning until noon, then he felt hungry. So he picked up his millet cake from where he had placed it between the roots of a tree. But, just as he was going to eat it he was taken aback: 'Eh! how was it that half of it had gone?'

He looked around him, behind and before, to the left and to the right, but not a sign of anyone could he find.

When he had finished eating, he went on with his work but with his mind on the strange happening.

'I'm the only person who comes here every day to cut brushwood for fuel. There's never been anyone else who has even come near the place. Whoever could have stolen and eaten half of my millet cake today?'

And he went on cutting and cutting. After a while he glanced behind him: 'Eh! Can I believe my eyes! I know I put what I cut this morning into a loose pile. Who on earth has tied it all up into bundles for me?'

---

1.   In Chinese, the title is a pun on the word *hsiang* which may be rendered 象 i.e. elephant or 相 i.e. Prime Minister.

人心不足蛇吞相

戊申二夏中吾繪

The Snake Will Swallow the Elephant

The more he looked, the more amazed he became. Finally, seeing that he had cut enough brushwood to make a load, he arranged the bundles into two equal halves, balanced each half on the end of his carrying pole, and set off for home with his load.

When Wong San got home, he told his mother all that had happened. She was also filled with amazement but she had the deeper wisdom which comes with old age, so she said to him,

'My son, don't tell a soul a single word of what has happened. Wait until tomorrow and see whether anything of the same kind happens again.'

The next day, Wong San went up the mountain to cut brushwood as usual, and the same strange things happened again. But this time, even while he was cutting, the handfuls of brushwood which he let fall at his back seemed to arrange and tie themselves into bundles as fast as he cut them. Handful after handful came together into a neat bundle. Then, at noon, when Wong San took his millet cake and looked at it, behold, half of it had gone!

I won't weary you with endless repetitions. It's enough to say that the same thing happened day after day, until one day Wong San was on the mountainside talking to himself and he muttered half-aloud, 'I still don't know who it is who comes here day after day and ties up the brushwood for me and eats half my lunch. Whoever you are, you should at least let me see you!'

Just as Wong San was uttering these words under his breath, he heard the sound of a cough behind him 'Huh! Huh!' A shiver went down his spine. He glanced behind him and saw

standing there a very old man with a white beard. Before
Wong San could utter a word, the old man chuckled and said,

'Young man, thank you for saving my life. If you had not
supplied me with your millet cake, day after day, at a time when
I was ill, I would surely have died of hunger.'

Wong San saw that the old man was a very kindly-looking
fellow and so was no longer afraid of him.

The old man told him that his dwelling was behind the
mountain, that his name was Sang and that, because he had been
ill for some time, he had been unable to go far afield to get supplies,
but, thanks to Wong San's millet cake, he had been able to survive.
He therefore asked Wong San to become his sworn brother, and
Wong San agreed to do so.

That evening Wong San told his mother all about the
white-bearded old man and their pledge to become sworn
brothers.

When his mother heard this she was very excited and
happy.

The next day Wong San's mother wrapped up two millet
cakes for him and told him to give one of them to his white-bearded
elder brother.

When Wong San reached his usual place on the mountainside he saw the white-bearded old man sitting amid the
protruding roots of a tree waiting for him. They greeted one
another and then immediately set to work cutting brushwood.
This time, the white-bearded old man helped Wong San in the
cutting, and my word, how swiftly he worked! Even though
Wong San used both hands without a moment's pause to tie
the brushwood into bundles, the little old man cut faster than
Wong San could bind. It took him more than three days to
carry away what they cut and bound in one. In one day,

Wong San earned much more than he had formerly earned in ten.

Day after day, the white-bearded old man helped Wong San to cut brushwood, and, because of this, Wong San and his mother became quite well off.

One day, some time after this, the white-bearded old man said to Wong San,

'Brother! we two have been as real brothers for some time now, and I have never once given you anything. Three days from now I want you to bring a knife with you to a cave which lies behind this mountain, and there I want you to cut out one of my eyes. Now, the eye is a very precious thing, so I want you to carry it to the capital and there present it to the emperor. In return he will give you an official position and from then onwards you and your mother will never be poor again.' When he had said this, the old man vanished.

That evening, Wong San's mother listened to what her son told her and then, after a moment's hesitation she cleared her throat and said,

'Huh! It's a rare thing to find a friend as good as that—a friend willing to cut out one of his own eyes in order to do us a good turn! But, in my opinion, it's better for us to depend upon cutting and selling firewood for a living than to cut out the eye of an elder brother.'

But Wong San was ambitious to gain an official position and so he did not listen to what his mother said. At noon on the third day he took a curved knife with him to the cave on the far side of the mountain and there he saw a big, long snake, in girth as big around as a wash-bowl. The snake raised its head, opened its mouth, closed its eyes and then slid across the cave.

But Wong San couldn't see his whitebearded elder brother anywhere.

Then the truth dawned upon Wong San.

'Ah! my former elder brother has been changed into a snake!'

Then he stepped forward, drew out his curved knife and savagely gouged out the snake's right eye. Then he wrapped up the eye in a piece of cloth and returned home.

Soon after this, Wong San journeyed to the capital where he presented his precious treasure to the emperor.

When the emperor looked closely at the gift he realized that it was a rare 'luminous pearl', for, as it lay upon his open palm it gleamed and glowed and gave light to the whole audience chamber.

He was so pleased with the gift that he conferred upon Wong San the rank of an official of the First Degree and appointed him to a position of authority second only to his own. He then gave the pearl to his beloved daughter, the princess.

The princess admired the pearl so much that she took it out every day to gaze at it as it lay upon her open palm. In so doing, she noticed that it was a male pearl. Ah! if only she could obtain the female pearl to match it—how wonderful that would be!

She dwelt upon that desire day after day from morning till night, so obsessed with longing for the pearl that she fell ill—so very ill that she lay at death's door.

When the emperor got to know about this he sent for his Prime Minister, Wong San, and said to him,

'If you can get another pearl to match the one you gave me, I will bestow my daughter, the princess, upon you in marriage.

Two matching pearls laid side by side: two matching persons joined in one.'

When Wong San heard this exciting offer he gave his whole-hearted promise to fulfil the emperor's wish. Carried aloft in his eight-bearer chair, he at once left the capital and, so displaying his military dignity and official rank, he returned to his home in the country.

When his mother saw that he had become Prime Minister she couldn't find words to express her joy. Still, she couldn't bring herself to agree that her son should cut out his sworn brother's remaining eye.

But Wong San was anxious to marry the princess and so refused to heed his mother's advice. Taking his jewelled dagger in his hand he set out for the cave which lay on the far side of the mountain.

When he reached the mouth of the cave he looked in and saw that the socket of his elder brother's eye was still drip, drip, dripping with blood while the other eye was streaming with sorrowful tears. And when Prime Minister Wong San called out 'Elder Brother!' his sworn brother merely nodded his head in reply. So Wong San continued,

'Elder Brother, if a man sets out to save another's life he should save it whole. If a man sets out to kill a person, he should not leave him half dead. I have now become Prime Minister, but I have not yet risen to be the emperor's son-in-law. To complete what you have begun, let me now cut out your right eye.'

And even while he was saying this, he drew out his jewelled dagger with the cruel and evil intention of gouging out his sworn brother's remaining eye.

But his elder brother merely cleared his throat and said, 'Huh! Very well.   Come on.   Cut it out.'

Wong San was very happy to receive this invitation: 'Ah! the princess is now mine!'

And so, gritting his teeth, he stepped forward to cut out the eye.

But, at that moment the elder brother could no longer put up with Wong San's attitude, so he opened his mouth, wide as a big charcoal brazier and, in a trice, swallowed down the Prime Minister.

That is why, when a man over-reaches himself, people say, 'The snake will swallow the elephant.'

THE DRUM THAT SHOOK HEAVEN

IN the Heavenly Palace there lived an Old Fairy who had seven grown-up daughters of whom the youngest was between seventeen and eighteen years old. He was very much afraid his daughters would turn their thoughts earthwards and, above all, that they would want to marry mortals, so he kept a strict eye on them. Every day, all day long, he made them exercise 'thought restraint' within the confines of the palace and never allowed them to visit anybody outside. His daughters, in this way, led a very secluded life and, in fact, they were bored to death.

Now the Old Fairy's youngest daughter, Seventh Sister, was a young woman of matchless beauty. One day, while she was resting, the sound of a flute, beautifully played by a human being, floated into her room. The tune was so beautiful that Seventh Sister was entranced by it and there and then decided to find out who the flautist was. So she secretly led her page-boy, a spotted deer, out of the room and together they peered down through the clouds.

It was Springtime, and the earth, clad with peachblossoms and green willows, was lovely to look upon. The Spring flowers were blooming, and the swallows were darting about in pairs.

Seventh Sister was lost in admiration. She gazed in the direction from which the sound was coming and there, she saw a handsome young farmer-lad, sitting under a willow tree playing his flute.

The Drum that Shook Heaven

The longer Seventh Sister gazed upon this young man the deeper she fell in love with him. She stood there entranced by what she saw.

The spotted deer, standing at Seventh Sister's side, immediately read what was in her heart and so whispered quietly to her, 'Seventh Sister, Earth is very lovely. If only we could visit it!'

When Seventh Sister heard these words she just nodded in agreement, so the spotted deer asked another question. 'Seventh Sister, you see that young man playing the flute down there. For some days now I have looked down and seen him cutting grass on the steep hillside. There's no doubt he's a very hard-working young man. Are you interested in him?'

Seventh Sister blushed, nodded her head, and said, 'How can I tell whether he is also good?'

The spotted deer replied, 'That's easy. Let me go down to Earth and put him to the test. Then you will know for certain.'

Seventh Sister at once gave her consent; and so the spotted deer sprang lightly upon a cloud, and descended to Earth.

Now the young man sitting under the willow tree, playing his flute, was called Wong San. His parents had died when he was still a baby and so, a lonely orphan, he earned his living by cutting grass on the mountain sides. On this day, he had just finished playing a tune, and was just standing up ready to get on with his grass-cutting when he saw a deer running straight towards him from the main road below.

The animal ran up to Wong San, put forward its two front legs and knelt before him and besought him saying, 'Big Brother Grass-cutter, save me! There's a wolf chasing me! Hide me, quick!'

Without giving the matter a second thought, Wong San agreed to do so by at once covering up the spotted deer with the half-dry grass he had cut. Then he himself climbed up into a tree.

Soon the wolf came along and saw Wong San up in the tree, and, panting heavily, said to him, 'Have you seen a deer go by here?'

Wong San pointed westwards and said, 'Yes, I saw one. It went off in that direction.'

So the wolf chased off towards the west.

When the wolf had gone, the spotted deer came out from under the heap of half-dried grass and thanked Wong San for saving its life. Then he started a conversation with Wong San, and began by asking him how many there were in his family, to which Wong San answered with a deep sigh, 'Alas! I rise up one person, I go to bed one person; there's only me, a tree without branches[1].'

The spotted deer then asked, 'Why don't you find yourself a wife?'

Wong San replied, 'Alas! who would want to marry a poor man like me?'

The spotted deer replied, 'Brother Wong San, don't let that worry you. Why should a capable, hard-working young man like you stand in need of a wife? Let me act as middle-man for you.'

Wong San replied, 'Thank you very much indeed.'

The spotted deer then said, 'It's getting late now. I'll serve you in that way another time. If you should need my help at any time, all you need to do is to call out three times towards the south-east "Elder Brother Deer" and I will come to your aid.'

---

1.   i.e.:   'I am all alone in the world, I have neither kith nor kin.'

As soon as the spotted deer had said this he disappeared in the twinkling of an eye. Then Wong San loaded his grass onto the two ends of his shoulder-pole and set off home with it.

The next day, Wong San got up at daybreak to cut grass. When he got as far as the river-bank, there he saw a young woman, dressed in pink, washing clothes at the river's brink. She was very beautiful. Her eyes were large and limpid. She was completely absorbed in her task with both hands busy washing and wringing the clothes, when suddenly, her feet slipped, and she fell into the river.

When Wong San saw this happen, without a moment's hesitation, 'Splash!' he plunged into the water and swam to her rescue.

The young woman, pressing and squeezing the water from her garments, thanked Wong San profusely saying, 'How good of you! Do you live anywhere near? May I go to your home to dry myself and my clothes in front of your fire?'

Wong San said that she could and so took her along to his home. And, when they got there, they found that the spotted deer was already there, waiting for them and holding in its mouth a change of new clothes for each of them. Wong San thought this was very strange, so he said, 'Elder Brother Deer, what brings you here?'

The spotted deer smiled and answered, 'To tell you the truth, I've come to act as your middleman. This young lady is the Seventh daughter of the Heavenly Palace household. She loves you for your hard-working character and your kind heart. She is willing to marry you. Are you willing to marry her?'

When Wong San heard the spotted deer ask this, he looked at Seventh Sister and his heart overflowed with joy. Glowing with happiness, he acknowledged his willingness. And so Wong San and Seventh Sister became man and wife.

The young couple worked very hard for their living and the spotted deer was their constant helper. In this way they passed their days in happiness and content.

But, when the Old Fairy learned that his daughter had married Wong San, he was furious. So, one day, when Wong San had gone out to work in the fields, he descended to Earth and, in a fuming rage, carried Seventh Sister back with him to the Heavenly Palace.

When Wong San got back home, he couldn't see Seventh Sister anywhere. He searched here, he searched there, he searched high and low the whole afternoon, and, when he still hadn't found her and was at his wits' end, he turned towards the south-east and called out, three times, in a loud voice, 'Elder Brother Deer! Elder Brother Deer! Elder Brother Deer!'

No sooner had he called out in this way, than the spotted deer stood before him and said, 'Brother Wong San, the Old Fairy discovered that you and Seventh Sister had got married and he was so furious about it that he has kidnapped her and carried her back to Heaven. And she is now a close prisoner in the Palace jail. She has, in secret, sent me to tell you what you must do.

'You are to sow a plot of ground with millet, and give it more care and attention than you have ever given to a millet-field before. Then, when harvest-time comes, pick out the strongest and tallest stalk of millet, don't cut it down when you reap the rest, and you will find that, in one night, it will shoot up until it reaches higher than the clouds. You will then be able to climb up this millet stalk and in that way reach the Heavenly Palace and Seventh Sister.

'And every day, at the same time, you must play upon your flute for Seventh Sister, and she, when she hears, will be able to endure her loneliness. Now whatever you do, don't forget. I have to get back now to look after Seventh Sister. I can't afford to linger any longer.'

When he had said this, he was gone in the twinkling of an eye.

When Wong San heard what the spotted deer told him, his heart was filled with anxiety. He gazed heavenwards, but all he could see was the unbroken ceiling of thick clouds. What hope had he of ever seeing Seventh Sister again? So he took out his flute and played a tune to comfort her.

He played it louder and more beautifully than he had ever played before, and the sound of the music travelled straight to the Palace jail where Seventh Sister was. And when she heard the sound of the flute, she felt that the cangue and the fetters were no longer as heavy or as tight.

Next, Wong San, in order to bring about his reunion with Seventh Sister as soon as possible, did exactly what she had told him to do. He sowed a plot of ground with millet and looked after it with more care than he had ever looked after a crop before. The millet grew, and was much better than any crop he had ever grown before; and Wong San rejoiced to see it.

Day after day, while the millet grew stronger and stronger, and taller and taller until the heads of grain began to fill out, Seventh Sister sat in the Palace jail waiting, day after day, for the grain to ripen. As for Wong San, while he too waited for the tall millet to ripen, every day seemed a year.

Day after day passed like this until Autumn came, and the millet ripened to a russet-red, and every head of grain looked as big as a broom-head. And among them stood one stalk of millet taller than all the rest. No one had ever seen the like before. No one had ever even heard of one to compare with it.

Wong San gathered all the harvest of his field into his store-room except the unusually tall, strong stalk. Then, during that night, that tall, strong millet stalk indeed shot up until it reached beyond the clouds. Wong San was overjoyed, and at once climbed up the millet stalk to Heaven.

Now, when Wong San reached the Heavenly Palace he saw, coming to meet him, six young ladies, all dressed alike in the same colour.

The eldest of the six asked him, 'Who are you? What do you want here?'

Wong San answered, saying, 'I'm Seventh Sister's husband. I've come looking for her.'

The six young ladies looked very pleased to hear this, and said, 'So you are our Seventh Sister's husband?'

Wong San replied, 'Truly, I am.'

Then the eldest one said to him, 'When we saw the millet was russet-red and ripe, we came here ready to meet you. Our Seventh Sister is still languishing, a prisoner in the Palace jail. And the spotted deer is also imprisoned there because he passed on to you the message she sent. For the time being you have no way of getting to see them. You must hide yourself . . . '

Before the eldest sister had finished speaking, the Old Fairy came, 'Clip-clop, Clip-clop', hobbling along with the aid of a staff. He pointed with his staff to Wong San and said to his daughters, 'Where did that human being come from?'

The Eldest Sister replied, 'He flew here from Earth, Father.'

The Old Fairy thought to himself, 'This young man must have some unusual powers, otherwise, how could he manage to fly here?'

So he said to Wong San, 'What have you come here for?'

Wong San replied, 'Respected father-in-law, I am the husband, sir, of your seventh daughter. Two things bring me here to the Heavenly Palace: first, to pay my respects, sir, to you, and secondly, to take Seventh Sister back home with me.'

When the Old Fairy heard this he was very angry, and said with a sinister chuckle, 'Ha-ha! So you are that farmer-lad, Wong San, eh?'

To which Wong San replied, 'Yes. I am.'

Then the Old Fairy quickly thought up an impossible task to set Wong San. He called for men to bring out a plough and then turned to Wong San and said, 'Seeing that you know all about farming, plough up all the weeds on the top of this wall for me. If you succeed, I will let you be reunited with your wife. If you fail, off you go!'

With these words, he clutched his staff, and, 'Clip-clop, Clip-clop', he tottered away.

Now, in ploughing a field, there was no one who was Wong San's equal, but, how on earth could he plough on the top of a wall? That was indeed a problem. Then Eldest Sister said to him, 'Husband of Seventh Sister, don't let it worry you. I will help you.'

Then she blew upon Wong San's feet twice, and at once Wong San became so light and so skilful that he was able to stand firmly on the top of the wall. Then, without the help of an ox to draw the plough, he quickly ploughed up all the weeds which were growing on the top of the wall.

Before long, the Old Fairy came back to see how he was getting on, and, when he saw that the weeds on the wall-top had already been ploughed up, he thought to himself, 'That's strange! That's strange!' This young man certainly knows a thing or two!'

Then another idea sprang into his mind of how to put Wong San to the test. So he called men to bring him out a bushel of powdered husks. Then he said to Wong San, 'Rub these powdered husks between your palms and make them into rope. If you can do this, I will let you be reunited with your wife. If you fail, then off you go!'

With these words, he clutched his staff and, 'Clip-clop, Clip-clop', he hobbled away.

Now in making rope out of hemp or out of any kind of straw, there was no one to equal Wong San. But how on earth could he roll powdered husks between his palms to make rope? That was indeed an impossible task. But the Second Sister said to him, 'Husband of Seventh Sister, don't let it worry you. I'll help you.'

On saying these words, she first blew once upon the powdered husks, then scooped up a handful and rolled it between her palms and began to make it into a rope which she handed to Wong San. He took over the task from her and, very quickly, he had soon rolled all the powdered husks between his palms and made them into rope.

Before long, the Old Fairy came back to see how he was getting on. All he could see was the finished rope, shiny and faultless; so he stood speechless.

Then he thought of another tricky problem to set Wong San. So he said to him, 'You've done well. Now go and rest awhile, for tomorrow, you must go to Monkey Mountain and

there steal for me the Heavenly Drum. If you succeed, I will
let you be reunited with your wife. If you fail, I will tell you
to be off!'

With these words, he clutched his staff and, 'Clip-clop,
Clip-clop', he hobbled away.

When the Old Fairy had gone away, Wong San was truly
at a loss as to what he should do, and thought to himself, 'How
on earth can I get hold of the Heavenly Drum?'

At that moment, Third Sister, Fourth Sister, Fifth Sister,
and Sixth Sister spoke together and said, 'Husband of Seventh
Sister, don't let it worry you. We'll help you.'

With these words, Third Sister took out a cotton sack, Fourth
Sister took out a small axe, Fifth Sister took out a flint, while
Sixth Sister took out a handful of sewing needles. They gave
these things to Wong San and told him exactly how to use them
in getting hold of the Heavenly Drum, and exactly what he should
do with it, once he had it in his hands. But they told him also
to be extremely careful, not to make a single slip, or it would cost
him his life.

When Wong San heard them tell of the difficulties he would
meet, his heart fainted for fear. But when he thought of rescuing
Seventh Sister, all fear left him.

The next morning, Wong San took up these four magic gifts,
said goodbye to his six sisters-in-law, and set out for Monkey
Mountain.

He eventually reached Monkey Mountain, and climbed up
by holding on to thorn-bushes and clambering up over loose stones,
and so made his way towards the top. His hands and feet were
cut and bleeding, and his clothes were torn to shreds, but he was
still undaunted, and pressed on towards the summit. He climbed
and climbed and, at last, he reached the top.

When Wong San got to the top of Monkey Mountain, he hid himself in a thicket. All he could see was a host of monkeys scampering about hither and thither. Then there, hanging from the branch of a big, leafy tree, was the Heavenly Drum with several monkeys standing on guard beneath it!

Next, Wong San went across to a muddy pool. There he scooped up mud which he plastered all over himself from head to foot. Then he sat on a stone to dry off in the sun.

Just at that moment, several monkeys came down to the muddy pool to bathe. When they saw Wong San they took him to be an idol fashioned out of mud and so they clumsily carried him aloft to a position beneath the Heavenly Drum, and there, they worshipped him.

Then all the monkeys wanted to bring offerings of food in worship of this new 'Mud Idol'. 'Bing-bang, Bing-bang', they scampered away, leaving behind a solitary old monkey to guard the Heavenly Drum.

When they were gone, Wong San took out the white cotton sack from inside his jacket, beckoned to the old monkey, and said, 'Quick! Come here!'

The old monkey, as if hypnotized, raced up to the cotton sack and then ran right inside it. Whereupon Wong San immediately pulled the drawstrings and tied up the mouth of the sack. Then, in a flash, 'Swish!', Wong San had climbed up the tree and had carried down the drum on his back, and, 'Ding-dang, ding-dang', he darted away with it.

The monkeys soon discovered what had happened, and, buzzing like a swarm of bees, they swooped after him. Wong San, 'Ding-dang, ding-dang', raced on ahead, while the monkeys, 'Bing-bang, bing-bang', scampered after him.

When Wong San turned his head and saw that the monkeys were gaining on him, he struck the ground behind him with his axe, and, immediately, a river with foaming currents appeared across the way and stopped the monkeys from truly catching up with him.

But, the monkeys, with a 'Splashety-splash' soon swam across the river and continued the chase.

Wong San raced on, 'Ding-dang, ding-dang, ding-dang!' while the monkeys chased after him, 'Bing-bang, bing-bang, bing-bang!' Then, Wong San turned his head and saw that they would soon catch up with him. So he took out his flint and threw it upon the ground. Immediately there rose up behind him a very, very high mountain which stopped the monkeys from truly catching up with him.

But, the monkeys clambered up and over the mountain and continued the chase.

Wong San raced on, 'Ding-dang, ding-dang, ding-dang!' while the monkeys chased after him, 'Bing-bang, bing-bang, bing-bang!' Then Wong San turned his head and saw that they would soon catch up with him. So he took out the handful of sewing needles and strewed them on the ground.

Immediately there rose up behind him a mountain covered with a forest of bright, sharp, gleaming swords which stopped the monkeys from truly catching up with him.

The swords which covered the mountain were so bright and gleaming, and their points so sharp, that the monkeys had no way of chasing after him any more.

After this, Wong San quickly returned to the Heavenly Palace where he saw Eldest Sister coming out to meet him. She took out and gave him two small balls of cotton wool and told him to plug his ears with them. Then she told him to get himself a short, stout stick.

Wong San did everything she told him to do.

Now the Old Fairy was gleeful when he had told Wong San to steal the Heavenly Drum, and he was just chuckling to himself, 'Ha-ha-ha! by this time, Wong San will surely be torn in shreds by the monkeys,' when Wong San himself turned up carrying the Heavenly Drum on his back!

When the Old Fairy saw Wong San standing there with the Heavenly Drum on his back, he was beside himself with rage, and decided to use the reverberations of the drum to shatter Wong San to death. So he said to Wong San, 'Let me try and see whether this is in fact the Heavenly Drum or not.'

Then he raised his staff and struck upon the drum with it. 'Bo-ong!!'; and at the sound, all the leaves of the trees came rustling down. And the Old Fairy thought to himself, 'That will certainly have stunned Wong San.'

But, who would have thought it! Wong San merely said, 'I didn't hear a sound. Strike it again; a bit louder, please!'

The Old Fairy was filled with amazement, and so struck the drum much harder than before, 'Bo-ong!!!'; and at the sound, 'Crr-ack! crr-ack! crack!!', all the buildings shook, and the Old Fairy thought to himself, 'That should have done the trick!'

But Wong San still felt nothing, and merely said, 'I didn't hear a sound. Strike it again, a bit louder, please!'

Now the two reverberations of the drum had made the Old Fairy so dizzy that he saw stars. So he hardly dared to strike the drum again. Then Wong San said, 'If you don't strike it, I will.'

And as he spoke, 'Bo-ong!!!' he lifted his short stout stick and suited the action to the words.

The effect was astounding. The noise shook both heaven and earth, and the reverberations killed off the wicked Old Fairy.

As soon as the Old Fairy was dead, Wong San opened the doors of the Heavenly jail, struck off Seventh Sister's cangue and fetters and, playing his flute, carried her back to Earth where they were united once more in their home.

The six sisters and the spotted deer also descended to earth to dwell among human beings, where each of the girls married a hard-working husband, and so everybody lived happily ever after.

The Fish-Ended Roof-Beam and the Earth-Heap Pavilion

THE FISH-ENDED ROOF-BEAM AND THE
EARTH-HEAP PAVILION

A very long time ago the people of a certain ancient hsien-city[1] wanted to build a beautiful and imposing Confucian temple. In order to make it a unique and magnificent structure some of them proposed that the main hall of the temple should be both lofty and wide with the main roofbeam made of a specially selected judas tree and that, at the rear of the main temple, they should build a Spring and Autumn Pavilion with a roof made out of a single piece of cinnabar. But where could they find such an enormous judas tree or a cinnabar rock of sufficient size? That was the problem.

After considerable discussion they decided to send men out to comb the surrounding countryside to seek and to buy the beam and the stone they needed.

The men searched everywhere for three months, but all in vain. They couldn't even find a pine tree of that size, never mind a judas tree! And as for the cinnabar rock, they couldn't even find a piece of granite that size.

Without either the giant roof-beam or the cinnabar rock for the roof they could not even begin; so those in charge of the construction were worried to death. They called several meetings and finally decided to put up wall-posters throughout the countryside offering a reward to anyone who could help them in their search.

---

1. a hsien: a district governed by a magistrate resident in the chief city or town of the hsien, called the hsien-city.

This plan produced results, for, in less than a month after the posters were put up, an old wood-cutter came forward and said, 'On the ninth peak behind the Western Mountains there is a judas tree so big that two men can scarcely touch hands around its trunk. It's not easy to find because it is overgrown from top to bottom with ferns and creepers. But I, from time to time, have cut some branches from it for firewood, and so I know it is a judas tree.'

Everybody was glad to hear this and immediately sent men to go with the woodcutter to find out whether what he said was true. They found that he had spoken the truth, so they gave him a big reward and sent men to chop down the tree and bring it back with them.

They say that it took four or five men a whole day just to cut down the tree and that they wore out an endless number of axes in doing so. And as for transportation, it took thirty men a whole fortnight to haul it to the city.

Some time after this, an old farmer came along and said, 'At the foot of the mountain beyond the Eastern Mountains there's a cinnabar rock as big as a house. It's not easy to find because it's completely overgrown with moss and lichen. But, on one occasion, I sharpened my knife on it; otherwise I wouldn't have known it was a cinnabar rock.'

Everybody was glad to hear this and immediately sent men to go with the farmer to find out whether what he said was true. They found that he had spoken the truth, so they gave him a big reward and sent men to bring the rock back to the city.

They say that it took every bit of eight hundred catties of jute rope merely to bind the rock, and that it took a hundred men a whole month to haul it to the city.

We can now say that everything was ready for the work to begin. But where could they find a master-builder to undertake such an enormous job?

In the whole city there were only two comparatively good builders, the one surnamed Chang and the other surnamed Wong. As far as workmanship was concerned, there was very little to choose between them, and each of them had a number of journeymen and apprentices. So people couldn't make up their minds which one to choose for the job. Finally, the only thing to do was to ask the local craftsmen and workmen to make the decision.

The local craftsmen and workmen discussed the matter and, because they were of one mind that Master Chang was senior to Master Wong and that he was an honest and conscientious master, they reached a majority decision that he should be put in charge of the whole construction. Now of course Master Wong was not very happy about their decision but he couldn't do anything about it. And so there the whole matter rested.

Master Chang had never before had experience of such a big contract so he was very excited about it. On the one hand he welcomed the chance to show people the quality of his workmanship, but on the other he was worried that he might overlook some small thing that would entirely spoil the whole undertaking. For this reason, from the very beginning, he paid meticulous attention to every detail of the construction. He supervised the workmen and personally made all the essential measurements. Whenever he came up against doubts or difficulties he went with proper humility to consult Master Wong and other craftsmen.

The contract was a very big one which required him to

employ between three and four hundred workmen, carpenters, stone-masons, plasterers and bricklayers, in addition to casual labourers. As the work proceeded, sometimes things went smoothly, but at other times difficulties cropped up. And why was this? Things went smoothly because all the materials needed lay ready to hand when construction started. Things didn't go smoothly because Master Wong was always creating trouble, not only by openly disobeying orders but also by playing dirty tricks behind Master Chang's back. But no matter what happened, Master Chang remained even-tempered and never made an issue of anything that Master Wong did. In this way, six months passed without any serious set-backs in the construction.

In a very short time the foundations were well laid, the walls took shape and the pillars were erected. They only needed to wait for the auspicious moment of the late-noontide hour of the fifteenth day of the eighth month to hoist the roof-beam and fix it in position. Then, just about ten days before the auspicious day dawned, Master Chang went to make a personal check of the exact measurements of the beam.

First of all, he checked the precise distance between the base of the two inside walls. But even when he had done this, he was not satisfied. So he climbed up to the top of the walls and there checked the measurements three times over. And every time he did so, the measurements proved to be exactly the same as those he had made in the first instance: that is, every time he measured, the distance turned out to be precisely seventy-seven feet and seven and seven-tenths of an inch. Satisfied on this point, he measured off the same length, seventy-seven feet and seven and seven-tenth inches, on the giant beam. This done, he checked these measurements three times over before he sawed off the surplus length from each end.

When he had done this, his anxieties were at an end, so he thought to himself, 'Now that's done, all I need do is to wait for the day when we can hoist the roof-beam into position. There's no chance now of any major mistake in the structure of the main hall.'

While all this was going on, the stone for the pavilion roof was being chiselled and shaped to its right size and was now ready. The four pillars, one at each corner, stood in position ready to support it. All the men needed to do was to wait to hoist it into position on the very day when the roof-beam would be raised.

But how could they ever hope to raise aloft such a heavy piece of solid stone? If they hired enough men to lift it, there wouldn't be enough room to stand. If they hired less men, the smaller team wouldn't have enough strength for the task. Besides, there were no men tall enough to lift it to the needed height. And if they decided to use poles, there were no poles strong enough to bear the weight. So what was to be done!

Master Chang searched his brains for a solution of the problem, but with no result. He went and consulted his craftsmen, but they couldn't suggest any solution of the problem either. Then he sought out Master Wong and asked his advice. But Master Wong, instead of giving advice, merely gave a supercilious reply: 'If the chief contractor can't solve the problem how can he expect me to know the answer!'

So Master Chang really didn't know where to turn for advice or how to solve his problem.

Day after day passed by and the date for raising the roof-beam drew nearer and nearer until there were only four days left before the fifteenth of the eighth month. And Master Chang was worried, on the one hand about how to raise the pavilion roof, and on the other about how to hoist the giant roof-beam. In his anxiety, in order to forestall any possible hitch on the crucial day, he took out his foot-rule and checked his measurements again. He was thunderstruck and almost frantic at what he discovered. He didn't know how it had come about but it was absolutely clear that the beam which had measured seventy-seven feet and seven and seven-tenth inches had shrunk to seventy-six feet in length!

With difficulty he mustered enough strength to stand. He wiped his brows in amazement and measured the beam yet again. Yes, it measured only seventy-six feet.

'Good Heavens!' he gasped, and collapsed, so shaken that a thousand stars swam before his eyes and he broke out from head to foot in a cold sweat. All he could do was to mutter over and over again, 'I'm finished! This time, I'm finished!'

Early the next day, one of his apprentices came to see him, and he couldn't help asking, 'The day I took the measurements of the beam, you were there, weren't you? Do you remember how many feet and inches we made it?'

The apprentice replied, 'How could I forget! That day I was the one who held the marking-line for you. The length was exactly seventy-seven feet, seven and seven-tenth inches, wasn't it?'

'That's strange! That's strange!' Master Chang kept on muttering this to himself over and over again.

'Master, what's the matter?' the apprentice asked.

'Well, when I went over yesterday to check the measurements the beam had shrunk by one foot seven and seven-tenth inches.'

'That's strange,' exclaimed the apprentice; and then added, 'It must be him! Indeed, he must be the fellow.'

'He? Who do you mean?'

'Master Wong. I'm absolutely certain that this is Master Wong's doing.'

When Master Chang heard these words, first he was shocked by them, and then he scolded his apprentice very severely, 'Don't suspect people unless you have grounds for your suspicion. Master Wong would never do a thing like that!'

'Master, don't be in too much of a hurry; please hear me out. Two nights ago I got up in the middle of the night to go to the toilet and I saw Master Wong hurrying away from the main hall in a very suspicious manner. And in his hand, he was carrying an axe and a saw. Then yesterday he was going about telling everybody he met that they'd now have a chance of seeing how "ingenious" you were.'

Master Chang was completely taken aback, but he controlled his temper and said in a mild voice, 'My lad, take care not to suspect others groundlessly. And what is more, don't go about slandering others. Master Wong and I are both old-established craftsmen. I don't believe he would play a dastardly trick like that on me!'

The apprentice felt very disturbed and aggrieved and turned to go away; and, as he was leaving, his master charged him several times over not to spread false tales abroad and, above all, not to go about slandering Master Wong. For the next two days Master Chang neither ate nor slept. Day and night he thought and thought and turned over in his mind all the problems he had met and solved in the long course of his business and all the experience and training his own master had passed on to him. But in spite of all his striving he couldn't think of any way of solving the problem of hoisting the beam and getting the roof aloft.

These two days and nights added ten years to Master

Chang's life. He became an old man overnight. He became thin and pale. He realized that there was only one more day left. The next day was the fourteenth. The day after that was the day set for hoisting the roof-beam and getting the roof aloft. What could he do about it!

In his misery Master Chang stared dreamily at the sky, and, as the sun sank slowly into the west his heart sank as surely into his boots. He wished he could drag the setting sun back from behind the mountains, back into the sky, so as to give himself a little more time to think through his problems.

Just then, an old man, gaunt and tall, and dressed in rags, appeared in the doorway. At his waist he carried an axe and a chisel, and announced that he was looking for the master builder in charge of the construction.

On hearing this, Master Chang hurried to the door and asked him, 'What's your business with the master builder?'

'I've come looking for work,' the old man replied.

'I'm the master builder here,' said Master Chang in reply, frowning sadly. 'Tomorrow will see the end of this job, so I can't very well take you on.'

'My friend, do try to help me out,' pleaded the old man. 'I've been out of work for months on end.'

To this plea, Master Chang replied in all sincerity, 'Under normal circumstances I would do my best for an old craftsman like you, but just now I truly can do nothing to help you. You little realize . . . . ai-ya! In a word, I don't want to keep you waiting and building on false hopes. You'd better look somewhere else for a job.'

'Why, what's wrong?' the old man asked.

'There's nothing the matter—there's nothing the matter.' And Master Chang frowned deeply.

The old man seemed to have detected Master Chang's hidden anxiety and so he once more pressed him to say what was worrying him. But Master Chang was entirely unwilling to say what was on his mind because he felt that he would not gain anything by telling; he would only place a burden of worry on someone else's shoulders.

Then the old man said, 'It will soon be dark. Can you let me sleep here tonight?'

'Yes, if you don't mind my giving you only a shakedown in my humble abode.'

Even while he was saying this he ushered the old man inside and, when he had invited him to sit down, said, 'I haven't yet asked your name. May I know it?'

'My surname is Yü, my given name Tsï.[1]'

'Have you had supper yet?'

'I haven't even had any breakfast today.'

On hearing this, Master Chang at once told his old wife to cook some rice while he himself took a basket and went to the market where he bought two carp. On his return, he gave them to his wife to fry.

When everything was ready, he hastened back into the room to keep the old man company.

How that old man Yü talked! He asked about this, that and the other. He asked how deep the foundations were, how high the walls were, why the main hall was so very broad and long, whether they had yet erected the pillars to support the roof of the pavilion which was to complete the design of the temple, and so on. It seemed as if he had an unusually clear conception of every detail of the construction.

---

1.   A witty division of the ideograph of the old man's name. He was soon to be identified as Lu Pan (魯班). He had divided his surname to give the upper half as 魚 (Yü), and the lower half as 日 (tsï).

As Master Chang listened he marvelled and was lost in admiration of his visitor's grasp of the details.   But when he remembered his own two unsolved problems he couldn't help venting a deep sigh.

It seemed as if Old Man Yü at that moment read exactly what was on Master Chang's mind, for he said significantly, 'My friend, it's no use worrying over a problem and keeping your worries to yourself.   Men in our line of business are bound to run up against difficult problems.   A man must be willing to think a problem through, and to go back over it again, with the certainty that he will eventually see what to do about it.'

Although the old man's words hit the nail on the head, Master Chang refrained from saying anything.

In a few minutes more the rice was cooked and the fish was fried ready to serve, so Master Chang invited Old Man Yü to sit in the place of honour at table.

When they were seated the old man said, 'I've been walking all day long today until my back aches and my legs ache too. If you could go and fetch me a little wine that would make your meal perfect.'

As soon as Master Chang heard this request he picked up the wine-jug and went out to buy some wine, and, on the way, he blamed himself for not having thought of the wine earlier. And at the same time, as he went along, the thought of the trouble with the beam and the roof, which he would have to face on the morrow, made a cold sweat break out on his forehead and trickle down between his shoulder blades.

When he got back home with wine, behold, Old Man Yü was nowhere to be seen and everything on the table was completely topsy-turvy!   Each of the fishes was resting flat on its belly across the top of a rice-bowl, and a chopstick was balanced from the open mouth of one fish across to the open mouth of the other, while on the opposite side of the table there was a heap of cooked rice and, resting upside down on top of it, was the big red bowl which had been used for serving up the fish.   When Master Chang lifted up the red bowl, he saw the tops of four chopsticks poking through the rice.   The rest of each chopstick, one in each corner to support the big red bowl, was embedded deep in the rice.

Master Chang was at first amazed when he saw this, but after giving it a moment's thought, it dawned on him what it all meant, so he dashed out of the house saying aloud, 'Aha! Now I know what to do!'

He rushed straight to the side of the main hall of the temple where the giant beam lay, picked up the two end-pieces which he had sawn off, took up his axe and chisel and fashioned each piece into the shape of a carp with its tail extended aloft and its mouth wide open.   Then, into the mouth of each carved fish he fitted one end of the beam.   Then, he took his ruler and measured from the gravitation point under the belly of one fish and along the beam to the gravitation point under the belly of the other fish; and he found that, without a fraction of an inch to spare, the distance was exactly seventy-seven feet and seven and seven-tenth inches.

Then, just as the dawn was breaking, he raced over to the site of the Spring and Autumn Pavilion and called together all the earth-carrying coolies and commanded them to take their carrying poles and bring loads of earth and first to pile it up all round the structure and then to fill up inside this earth-circle to form a mound which would reach to within a short distance of the top of the four pillars.

By the time Master Chang had seen to it that all this was done, the auspicious moment of the noontide hour had arrived, and so, to the accompaniment of firecrackers, the giant beam was hoisted into position and behold, it fitted exactly! At the same time, a team of men harnessed their carrying poles to the cinnabar roof and, bearing its weight from their shoulders, they walked steadily up the earthmound and placed the roof securely into position.

Master Chang was so excited about all this that the tears streamed down his cheeks and he kept on murmuring, over and over again the old man's advice, saying to himself, 'He was right! A man in our line of business must be willing to think a problem through and to go back over it again and again, with the certainty that he will eventually see what to do about it.'

As for Master Wong, while people were still applauding Master Chang's success, he, shamefaced and with a hang-dog look just sneaked away.

Afterwards, it was rumoured Old Man Yü was none other than Lu Pan; and people called that giant beam The Fish-Ended Roof-Beam, and they called that particular pavilion The Earth Heap Pavilion.

THE BEGGAR DEFEATS THE PROFESSIONAL BOXER

(Part of a Long Sequence of such *Wu Hsia* Tales)

. . . Teh Yuan muttered an answer and, after eating his lunch, changed his long outer gown, hid a sword inside it, and walked out at the West Gate of the city alone.

When he came to the Wu Hou Temple[1] he noticed a beggar lying on the ground in front of the entrance. The beggar was lying on his back with his face towards the sun and seemed to be sound asleep.

Teh Yuan was somewhat surprised at the sight. It reminded him of the fight he had with the gang of thieves on the river bank near North Temple Confluence and how, when he had been almost downed by the attackers there had come, all of a sudden, from the midst of the mountains, a flash of silver light which had prevented the robbers' weapons from wounding him, and how, in that flash of light he had caught a faint glimpse on the mountain-side of the figure of a beggar.

Teh Yuan had not forgotten that experience, so he now stepped nearer to examine the beggar more closely and found that his hair was tousled like hay, his complexion pale like tallow, his stature dwarf-like, and that even on that autumn day he was wearing an unlined, blue cotton gown which was grimy and smelly with dirt and sweat. He noticed too that there was something

---

1. Wu Hou Ssǔ: A Temple on the outskirts of Chengtu, the capital of Szechuan, which contains in its precincts the grave-mound of Wu Hou, a famous prime minister of the period of The Three Kingdoms.

The Beggar Defeats the Professional Boxer

extraordinary about his skinny, brown legs, and also about his finger nails which, all ten of them, were more than three inches long and the colour of white jade.

While Teh Yuan stood pondering over what he saw he heard the sound of approaching hoofs. Turning his head he saw someone coming on donkey-back. The rider who dismounted was none other than Snow Butterfly.

Snow Butterfly recognised Teh Yuan as he moved towards her and was about to speak to her when, suddenly, the leaves on the tree-top overhead rustled and a voice cried out 'Help! or this poor beggar will be smashed into meatpaste!'

The sound had hardly died away when there came a loud crackling noise from the topmost branches, and, from the top of the cypress tree, as if from the sky, down rolled a man like a huge meat ball!

All the trees that grow around Wu Hou Temple grow seventy or eighty feet high and are thousands of years old. This particular tree was especially old and some of its branches stretched out a hundred feet. Anyone who fell from the top, no matter how skilful he might be at landing, would be bound to sustain internal injuries or to be crippled. But this man twirled down from above like a windmill, then, as he neared the ground, jerked his body round a little and stood up unhurt!

Teh Yuan first stared at the new arrival in amazement and then realized that he was the selfsame beggar who had been sleeping at the entrance of the Temple.

Snow Butterfly had never dreamt that such a man could have been hiding in the tree top. She had arranged with Teh Yuan to meet him there that day in order to have a few private words with him; and now this uninvited guest had suddenly dropped from the skies and interrupted the assignation.

The lady was very annoyed, but the beggar was so unaware of her embarrassment that he addressed himself to Teh Yuan: 'Honourable Sir, thanks to you I am still alive! I am only an old beggar! I am eighty-two years old! I don't know what sins I committed in my previous incarnation that I am now condemned to suffer this life of penury! This very day I intended to cast myself down from this treetop to finish myself off, to make an end of all my sufferings, but thanks to you, I am still alive. This shows that the Lord of the Underworld is not yet ready to let me render up my account to him. I am only a poor beggar. I have no skills. All I can do for a living is to cast horoscopes and tell true fortunes by phrenology. You sir, have a remarkable cranium; and I can see that this lady will marry a man of rank and distinction—she will surely marry a nobleman of the first rank.'

Teh Yuan listened with amusement to the beggar's crazy rambling on at other people's expense and was just going to speak when Snow Butterfly, her face suffused with shyness and annoyance, burst out, 'Hold your tongue, you rogue! What are you getting at? This is Szechuan, and people here are prosperous, and have always been so. Doubtless there are beggars here but they are not half-starved ghosts like you. Now, my good man, don't try to put anything over on me. Out with the truth.'

The beggar raised his eyebrows, grimaced, then laughed outright and said. 'Indeed, my lady, you are not far from the truth. In Szechuan beggars have well-organized beggars' guilds for mutual aid, so every last one of them is well nourished. But my case is different. Neither the big guilds nor the small ones will assist me. I've had nothing to eat for three days, so my hunger-pangs are now unbearable. That's why I climbed to the

top of the tree, for there I could at least eat my fill of the
North-East wind.   But when I saw you two down below I lost
my foothold and so came toppling down.   The fall hasn't finished
me off but it has twisted my insides into a state far worse than
the pains of death.   In the name of the merciful Kuan-Yin, good
madam, pity me!'

Having spoken thus, he burst out laughing and continued,
'If Madam would like to know my name, I will tell her, for I do
have one, it is Tu Chung-k'u—Griping Belly Ache—for I do not
belong to any beggars' guild and so I receive no benefits.   Therefore, good lady, be generous and your reward will be many blessings,
a long life and a quick succession of twelve sons.'

These words of the beggar roused Snow Butterfly's annoyance
even further.   To think of it! she, an unmarried girl, being
addressed as Madam and matron.   She first blushed to the very
ears with overwhelming embarrassment and then grew angry.
Next she plunged her hand into her pocket, drew out a few
small silver coins, held them in her palm, and then, 'Sh-Sh-!!',
she hurled them like arrows which sped like a flash of silver straight
to the beggar's left temple, saying as she hurled the coins, 'If you
need money, catch these!'

As for the beggar, he quite leisurely stretched out a skinny
hand, and, with one turn of his wrist, caught the coins between
his fingers.   Then he laughed aloud, saying, 'Thank you, kind lady.
This will suffice to buy me at least three catties of dogmeat.'

When Teh Yuan realized that the beggar had managed to
catch the coins by listening to the wind, he determined to
demonstrate his own skill, so he took out two copper coins, held
them in the palm of his hand and, using a spear-hurling technique,
with one movement of his right hand, 'Bang-Bang!' he aimed the
coins directly at the beggar's eyes.

The beggar calmly opened his lips and caught the coins in his mouth. Then he opened his lips again and dropped the two coins into the palm of his hand.

'Ha-ha!' he laughed. 'Very good, very good! Thank you, thank you! May you, Sir, and your good lady be blessed with countless descendants of princely rank. Long life and happiness be yours! As for me, I'm off to buy me some wine. Pardon me for leaving you now!'

With these words he sprang upwards like a hawk, soared some fifty or sixty feet into the air, hovered awhile, then floated up and down three or four times and was gone.

Snow Butterfly looked in amazement beyond the grove of trees, restrained herself for a moment and then exclaimed, 'Goodness me! what a blunder! That was one of the Immortals!'

Teh Yuan smiled and replied, 'It was indeed. That beggar was no mere human. He's the very man who helped me that night on the river bank at North Temple Confluence to make my escape from the rascally trap laid for me by those bloodthirsty villains.'

At this, Snow Butterfly brightened up. 'Ah,' she said, 'so that's the man, eh? If so, then the three Knights Errant of Ch'in Ling[2] must be here!'

Teh Yuan interrupted her, 'Who on earth are the three Knights Errant of Ch'in Ling?'

Snow Butterfly replied, 'For many a year these three have been well-known throughout the length and breadth of Szechuan. The first of them is the monk Liu Fan, the second is the beggar Liu Kung-fu, and the third is the commercial traveller Hsu Fei. All three of them have great prowess in wrestling and they

---

2.   The traditional mountain home in South Shensi of the fabulous heroes of Szechuanese folk-lore.

frequently disguise themselves and move among men, helping the weak against the strong and acting in a spirit of universal benevolence. In Szechuan there are many corrupt officials, local bullies and dishonest village elders all of whom hate the three Knights Errant like poison but they cannot do anything about it.

'As for that beggar who was here just now, he gave his name as Griping Belly Ache—Tu Chung-k'u. The name rhymes with Liu Kung-fu! He can be no other!—the beggar knight errant Liu Kung-fu himself! What a pity I didn't realize it while he was here. I must have eyes and no eyes[3]. What a chance I've missed!'

At this thought, Snow Butterfly stamped her feet and sighed while Teh Yuan stood dumb with amazement. Finally Snow Butterfly found words to express her feelings, 'If the Venerable Sage Liu is here there must be some good reason for his presence. Maybe he is going to be one of those taking part in the Feats of Strength Challenge Contest to be held in the courtyard of the Three Officials' Temple.'

The couple then chatted together until they were once more inside the city walls of Chengtu.

*   *   *   *   *   *

Two days later, Teh Yuang and Snow Butterfly rode out together to Three Officials' Temple to see the contest between the Mount Hua School and the Ming River School.

Three Officials' Temple lies about ten miles outside the East Gate of Chengtu. Everywhere on the road to the Temple crowds of people, men and women, young and old, streamed along to see the Challenge Contest.

---

3.   The Chinese, literally translated: 'Like, having eyes but being unable to see the Big Mountain (i.e. T'ai Shan).

In the front courtyard of Three Officials' Temple there was a mound of yellow earth and, about halfway up it, was the platform on which the contest was to be staged.

On looking more closely, Teh Yuan and Snow Butterfly saw that the platform was about eighty feet square and that it was supported by seven or eight pinewood posts each the size of a wassail bowl in circumference and each about six feet high[4]. The four sides of the platform were draped with red and green silk hangings and paper decorations in the shape of balls and flowers.

About thirty feet away from the platform, and a little above it, was a bamboo mat shed festooned with paper decorations and lamps. Across the front of the mat shed was suspended a signboard on which were inscribed in gold the four characters 'Through Strength Friends Meet,' each character the size of a bushel measure. Under the shed were three banks of tiered seats for spectators.

As the hour was still early there was no one on the platform, so Teh Yuan and Snow Butterfly had a clear view of the wooden stands erected upon it for holding the eighteen different weapons to be used in the contest, each weapon gleaming brightly and reflecting the sunlight.

Around the platform itself a very large crowd was already gathering. People were jostling and bumping into one another while hawkers elbowed their way back and forth through the crowd selling candy and other tasty delicacies. The chanted cries of the hawkers made the place sound like a fairground.

Teh Yuan and Snow Butterfly also noticed particularly the benches provided on opposite sides of the platform as waiting

---

4.   The Chinese reads 'sixty feet'; an exaggeration, or a slip, on the part of the
      story-teller.

places for the contestants. The benches on the East side, designated for the Ming River School were occupied by only four or five people, but those on the West side reserved for the Mount Hua School were quickly filling with contestants, both monks and laymen, and in their midst a strange monk of gigantic stature. He had a head like a leopard, a face like a tiger and huge jowls like a lion. All in all, his appearance was terrifying and dominating.

He was clad in a much-patched purple robe, and, hanging at his back, he carried a long-handled ladle, its bowl the size of a duck egg. On his feet he wore straw sandals with hempen soles. Anyone looking at him couldn't help feeling that he might be the Golden Buddha himself come among us from the Temple, or that even one of the Lo-Han[5] had come into our midst.

On his left stood a dark-complexioned middle-aged fellow with a forbidding, military bearing and bushy, overhanging eyebrows that glistened like a tiger's. He was wearing a black brocade jacket and a pair of thin-soled running shoes.

These two were the chief contestants for the Mount Hua School.

The other members of the team, more than thirty in number, were all powerfully built fellows, some tall, some short, some fat, some thin, all variously dressed. Anyone could tell at a glance that they were from the mountain-region of the province.

Teh Yuan and Snow Butterfly first looked at these men and then turned their attention to the centre back of the stage, where they could see, to the right and to the left, two wooden red-lacquered, notice-boards upon which notices had been carved in gilded characters.

---

5. The sages, or saints, of the Buddhist paradise.

That on the left was inscribed with the usual official proclamations and announcements to which no one paid much attention, but that on the right was inscribed with the rules governing the contest such as: 'In Single Combat—Two against One is an Infringement', 'In Knock-Out Contests—the Use of Hidden Weapons is Prohibited', and so on.

While Teh Yuan was scanning these rules, suddenly, the people standing round the stage roared out, 'Here comes the Ming River School Team!'

Teh Yuan and Snow Butterfly turned around and saw five or six members of the Ming River Team were arriving on the scene.

The first comer was a fat-faced, bullet-headed monk, short, powerful and thick-set. The next arrival was the selfsame beggar—the ragged bag of bones who had teased them at Wu Hou Temple. But the third arrival was the strangest of all. He was wearing a long gown with a black brocade sleeveless jacket and a small skull-cap. He had hollow cheeks, a pasty complexion and a moustache which drooped like the twin bracts of a water-chestnut. He wore a pair of white, baggy calico stockings and a pair of outsize slippers. With toes turned well out, 'Slip-slop, slip-slop', he strutted along carrying an iron abacus in his left hand.

Teh Yuan almost laughed outright, 'Are these indeed the three famous Knights Errant of Ch'in Ling!'

The disreputable beggar, sallow and bony, seated himself on the front bench of the Ming River School Team and sat there, stretching and yawning.

On seeing this behaviour, Snow Butterfly whispered to Teh Yuan, 'Look, my friend, look there! There on that bench sit the three Knights Errant of Ch'in Ling! We've already made the acquaintance of the beggar. The corpulent monk must be Liu Fan. And the one with long gown and the skull-cup can be none other than Hsu Fei, the commercial traveller of the famous trio!'

While the two were whispering about this, a sudden roar of fire-crackers burst out upon the stage: 'Bang! Bang! Bang!'. And when the noise died away, the whole front of the platform was littered deep with the shredded red paper of exploded firecrackers.

After this, one of the huge tall fellows of the Mount Hua Team, the one who had been sitting next to the outlandish monk, stood up and stepped forward. He was swarthy-complexioned and, by that time, had changed into a colourful costume and, in his left hand, was rolling together some iron walnuts which made a rasping sound as he ground them against his palm. He was none other than the Champion of the Mount Hua School and the Master of Ceremonies of the whole contest. His name was Yao Kai-tai, nicknamed Little Fire God.

As soon as he stepped forward he immediately took hold of his own hands at full arms' length and bowed ceremoniously to spectators on all four sides of the stage in turn, saying as he bowed, 'Friends and members of the audience! My illustrious teachers have entrusted my unworthy person with the task of organising the Autumn Contest. Our Szechuan has always been the nursery of spirited wrestlers, so this kind of contest is held annually, and every year we discover, through the contest, several outstanding champions. But this year's contest between the Mount Hua and the Ming River Schools is being held to decide who shall control the Toh River Wharf. You all know only too well the rights and wrongs of the dispute[6] so I do not

---

6.   Lit.: 'Those who face the lamp and those who face the fire.'

say anything more about it here, for, friends and neighbours, there are those among you who side with one group and those who side with the other. In any case, the verdict will come from those who are now on this stage. The decision will be given on man to man trials of strength. So, with no more ado, will the honourable contestants please step forward. We live our lives only once. Look well and you will see the sight of a lifetime!'

When he had thus spoken he repeated his ceremonious bows to the audience, turned his back upon them and jumped down from the stage to the accompaniment of thunderous applause from the Mount Hua benches.

No sooner had he jumped down than, out from the Mount Hua Team's dressing room, there issued forth a blue-clad figure. He had the haunches of a monkey and the shoulders of a tiger and he strode firmly like a dragon. This personage mounted the stage, stood on the front edge of it and shouted at the top of his harsh, throaty voice, 'Listen to me, all of you! My name is Kiang Shih. From my early boyhood I have trained myself to develop a cranium of iron strength. I am now known everywhere as Kiang Shih of the Irong Skull. I am here today to contest the first round for the Mount Hua School. Now, which of you friends over there would care to step forward to meet me in the first round!'

He had hardly finished speaking when, shadowy and light as a ball of cotton-wool and swift as a bird in flight, a man, his form scarcely distinguishable, circled the spectators on three sides, alighted on the stage and then spoke in a childish treble, 'And so you are Kiang Shih of the Irong Skull, eh? How would you like me to pummel you into Kiang Shih of the Bean-Curd Skull?'

When he spoke, those on the stage and those in the audience, some thousands altogether, stared in amazement! The person who had alighted before them was a strange-looking little fellow. Indeed he was none other than the beggar who, a moment before, had been sitting on the front row yawning.

He looked about twelve or thirteen years old. He had a mop of tousled hair his face was covered with greasy dirt, and his piercing, staring black eyes gleamed revealing their whites. His garment, which was short and dirty, was much-patched and tattered and was held in at the waist by a girdle of plaited straw.

His legs and feet were bare except for a pair of stinking straw sandals, and he was so pale and scraggy you would have thought he had had nothing to eat for at least three days. By contrast, Kiang Shih of the Iron Skull towered above him like a tall black pagoda, like a threatening black cloud brooding high over Hell far beneath it.

Everybody in the audience roared with laughter and surprise, wondering whether hunger had made the young beggar crazy. As for Iron Skull Kiang, he stood dumbfounded. He just stared at the young beggar who seemed so puny that a puff of wind might have blown him away, and thought to himself, 'Even if I vanquish the puny beggar at one blow, folks in the audience will only deride me!' So he quickly said aloud, 'Heh, you young beggar! If you want to beg for rice, do your begging down below among the audience. What do you think you're doing here? Do you mean to beg for certain death?'

Scarcely were the words out of his mouth when the little beggar suddenly sprang about six feet into the air and gave Iron Skull Kiang a quick and resounding punch on both sides of his head. Irony Skull Kiang, in spite of his bravado, could not dodge the blows on his temples. While he still was seeing stars, the little beggar mocked at him, 'Bean-Curd Skull! That will teach you to despise me!'

At this, all present burst out laughing, all except Iron Skull Kiang, who with an angry roar rushed forward towards the little beggar and tried to deliver a strong blow, right and left. The left was a rapid feint, but the right was aimed at his opponent's chest, like a panther's paw at its victim's heart.

But the little beggar was very agile. He lowered his right shoulder, gave a half turn and then, quick as lightning, darted to his opponent's rear where he lifted his right foot and kicked him on the behind. But, because Iron Skull Kiang had punched the empty air with the full force of his strength he staggered forward a few steps and so did not receive the full force of the little beggar's kick—otherwise he would surely have toppled over. But fortunately he was a trained wrestler, and so, when his blows encountered the empty air, he had immediately put the other foot forward in order to recover his balance. Thus it was that he received only a glancing kick on the behind. Even so, he lost his balance, staggered three or four more steps forward, and was lucky not to have fallen over.

With one voice the audience rocked with laughter, 'Ha-ha-ha!'

Meanwhile the little beggar stood stock-still on one side and taunted Iron Skull Kiang, 'Bean-Curd Skull! Don't worry! I don't intend to rob you of your cur's life! I only want to make you dog-tired and then I will shame you before the assembled company.'

At this, Iron Skull Kiang, panting like a tired bull, bellowed, rushed forward, and, with his two fists, rained blows directly upon the little beggar. But, who would believe it, the little beggar, in spite of his diminutive size, displayed remarkable agility. He managed to dodge every blow by darting first to the right, then to the left, then to the front, then to the back of his opponent, like a dancing shadow-puppet around the shade of a lighted lamp.

Iron Skull Kiang drew upon his last reserves of strength. Even so, he failed to harm even one hair of the little beggar's head, but, like an infuriated bull, he expended all his strength in vain. This too made everybody in the audience roar with laughter.

Teh Yuan and Snow Butterfly could not help laughing too.

After thirty or more rounds of this kind, Iron Skull Kiang was dripping with sweat, but the little beggar darted to the front of the stage and stood there, on the very edge, making faces at his opponent and laughing outright, 'Ha-ha-ha!'

At this, Iron Skull Kiang roared like thunder, lowered his head and, husbanding his last ounce of strength, took up the stance of an infuriated bull in a bull-ring and drove his iron skull at the little beggar's body expecting that with one impact he could knock him inside out and finish him off.

No one could have guessed what the little beggar intended to do in order to shame his opponent. When he saw the iron skull driving towards him he sprang nimbly three feet to the left, with the result that Iron Skull Kiang gored the empty air, could not check his own impetus, and so, when the little beggar gave him a kick on the behind, he continued as if in flight some twenty-feet beyond the front edge of the stage and then crashed powerless to the ground like a flying kite when the string is severed.

Ho Wai-Kwan's Vigil

HO WAI-KWAN'S VIGIL

(Sung to 'South Tune' with zither accompaniment)

I.   I lean upon my balcony
Gazing towards the eastern rim of heaven
Yearning for my beloved.
My tears flow freely as I think of him.
Lonely I recall our sad leave-taking.

The Milky Way on starry nights
Sunders wide the Cowherd and the Weaving Maiden.[1]
Sundered far is my dear love from me.

Fragrant flowers swiftly fade and die, my love.
'Twas ever thus.
And I have fears
My Springtime years
Will die before you come again to me.

The hand of Time will not be stayed while you
Linger on an alien shore
Loitering there to cull
Soon-fading blossoms and sallow willow fronds.[2]
Come home, come soon, my love, to me.

---

1. According to Chinese mythology, the Cowherd (Altair in the constellation Aquila) and the Spinning Maiden (Vega in the constellation Lyra) fell devotedly in love, but angry relatives, who had other plans for them, condemned them to live separated on either side of a broad river (The Milky Way). However, in spite of the injunction they managed to meet once a year at the conjunction of the two constellations on the 7th day of the 7th lunar month.

2. Poetic terms for tea-girls and prostitutes.

Beautiful Wei Hsün, Hsiang Yü away,
Grieved long alone
And nobly wept her whitening hair.
So I, the like case mine,
Sad mourn till your return.

II. The watchman on his nightly round
With gong-beats sounds
The first watch of the night.
The moon, new risen,
Begins its journey to its setting.

Fear grips my heart
When low among the orchard trees
I hear the solitary cuckoo call
Beneath the blossom-laden peach tree boughs:
'Cuck-coo! Cuck-coo!'

At every call
My heart's blood mingles with my falling tears.
Each cuckoo's cry
Echoes my heart's call to you:
'Come home! Come home!
Why stay! Why stay!'

Could my heart's sighs
Attain your dwelling place
Day and night,
Night and day...
My voice you'd hear:
'Come home! Come home!
My love, come soon!'

And you would heed; and in your arms,
In joy surpassing words,
My pleading tears would cease to flow.

No more would the shrike and the swallow
Fly their separated ways to East and West.

But woe is me!
For I well know
Strong, far-stretching lotus roots will not suffice
To bind your wandering heart to mine.
Fragrant blossoms left ungathered fall
And soon lie dead upon the chilly Springtime earth.

(Change to 'The Wild Plum Blossom' Tune)

III. The watchman on his nightly round
With gong-beats sounds the hour,
The second watch of my long night.
The moon shines bright upon my casement.
I need no lamp to show me
My fading beauty and my greying hair
My bridal kerchief soaked with my sad tears.

Thoughts of you are like cool autumn waters
Lapping quietly against the sun-dried reeds.
Renounce your wanderings and return, my love.

When people here remember thy carefree, happy ways
They speak in one breath of Tu Mu[3] and of thee

---

3. Tu Mu: also known as Mu Chih (牧之) a minor poet of the T'ang Dynasty
who was referred to as Hsiao Tu (小杜) i.e. the Lesser Tu Fu. Tu Fu
(杜甫) was the famous poet of the T'ang period.

And when they do,
Gay occasions come crowding to my mind
As when in happier days we feasted with our friends
And flushed with wine
We two outwatched the night.
And pointing here to my Red Gabled Room
You whispered low to me,
'My true love dwells under that roof tree.'

How little weight I gave your laughing words.
But now I weep my green-clad cavalier.
When shall I have again the heart to play
My p'i-p'a[4] while you bend to hear?

IV. The watchman on his nightly round
With gong-beats sounds
The third watch of the night.

The rounded moon sails high above the cassia trees.
On such a night as this we hired a boat
And floated gently under Su Chü Bridge[5],
Pearly in moon light.
You played the p'i-p'a while I sang to your tunes.
Then I played the flute to accompany your singing.
Gaily we vowed to be true—
True vows that death alone would end.
How can you forget those sacred vows?

Nor Heaven nor Earth can e'er forgive
Your fickle breaking of your plighted troth.

---

4.   A three-stringed instrument something like a guitar.
5.   A bridge near Canton.

The gods themselves with deathless hate
Avenge my sorrow-laden heart.
While you remain unmoved, uncaring,
'Tis meet I cast my wretched, ended life away.

V. The watchman on his faithful round
With gong-beats sounds
The fourth watch of the night.

The full-orbed moon floats on beyond
The bronze-tinged pallisades.
I weep alone and mourn my absent love.

The Faithful Maid, long turned to stone[6],
Awaits age-long her lord's return.
Your Faithful Maid looks out across the bay
To Fu Yung Beach
To Lai Ch'i Bay[7] where you once dwelt.

Across the tide my straining eyes
Scan long in vain for you.
My daily letters,
All for you,
Remain unsent.

(Change tune to the Major Key)

VI. The watchman on his nightly round
With gong-beats sounds
The fifth watch of the night.

---

6. The Faithful Maid: The Amah Rock in Shatin Valley near Kowloon.
7. Lai Ch'i Wan — a bay near Canton.

The bright moon shines across upon the eastern wall.
I lean upon my latticed balcony,
In garments light and thin.
I shiver with the burden of my thoughts of you.
My shoulders tremble in the chill dawn wind
If only we each could change into a phoenix
And fly far far away
To meet united on some distant fabled moonlit shore.

But the mandarin duck awakens sharply from
      its drowsy dream[8]
A dream in which I saw, so clear
The Ocean Pearl Tower receive again
The Sea Foam Bell.[9]

I drag myself to my awakening.
With slow and heavy strokes I brush my hair.
I see the sun's disc red and round
Shines through my bamboo window blinds.

---

8.   The mandarin duck and drake: the traditional symbols of enduring wedded happiness.
9.   A famous tower which formerly stood on an island in the Pearl River. The bell has long disappeared. Of the tower, only the name now remains as a street-name.

THE LOVER TO HIS FORMER MISTRESS

The Lover (*1st Phrase: Irregular Rhythm*)
> I gaze up at Ch'in Huai Lodge
> (*Another Tune*)
> I hope my former sweetheart is at home
> And well.
> (*Slow Rhythm: 'River Tune'*)
> The willow fringed banks
> The scenes of our past love
> Are blotted out in mist and rain
> I come alone, your former lover,
> While the wind is moaning in the stormy night.
> (*Tremulo*)
> Even when I see again the lamplight glow
> Gleaming faintly for me still
> From the Red Chamber of my lady love
> I know our former love is past
> Broken and gone.
>
> I tap lightly on her rosy lacquered door
> And while I do
> My heart beats fast
> And flutters like a hunted deer.

The Lady (*Tune: 'The Three-Legged Stool'*)
> I open the door ajar
> To ask more carefully
> Who might my midnight caller be.

風塵情侶

丙申吉公于港島戊申年夏

The Lover to His Former Mistress

Indeed it is a new-made man of rank
Comes knocking at my door.

Forgive me if my heart receives so coldly now
The Prime Minister's handsome son-in-law
My former sweetheart.

You a new-made bridgegroom
Surely seek me here mistakenly!

The Lover (*Regular Rhythm*)

Every word you utter in contempt
Pierces me with your hate
And cold despising.

I long ago explained my case to you.
Why do you now receive me thus
Without a chance to tell you why
Our case is altered so?

Give me a brief chance, I pray,
To speak with truth
What has befallen me.

Your cheeks are lovely as peach-blossom
Newly opened,
But your manner is sternly forbidding
Frosty-cold.

They say, whenever old friends meet
Joy reigns.
I little dreamt to have at my coming
Reproach and tears.

People who send forth husbands to win
Official position and honours
Do so regretfully—
But you spurred me on, bade me compete,
To strive for honour and preferment.
Before our wedding day,
You urged me on the path to high success.

I have fulfilled your highest hopes of me
And now return.
My name stands high upon the pass-list,
But out alas!
Men in authority have power to compel
Those who succeed.
I myself, truly, never sought in any way
This high marriage
Linking me to the Prime Minister's family
Where my heart was not.

The Lady (*Tune: 'The Two Kings'*)

You have gained the notice of the great ones,
Your name stands high upon the pass-list,
Enrolled in honour.

Many, ah many a girl like me
Has been forsaken,
Left, in favour of another
High in birth and fortune.

But I, who have no fortune in my face or life,
Now blame myself for building up high hopes
Of your return to me.

Why should a Chang T'ai lady of pleasure
Hope to set herself
To vie with the prize of a Prime Minister's daughter!
How could I, a prostitute, have charms
To hold you all life long till you are old?

The Lover (*Tune:'Hungry Horses Shake Their Harness Bells'*)
Will you not forgive me?
Every word you speak
Weighs heavy with reproach.
You tell me I reject your love,
You blame me for forsaking you
And turning my heart to another.
Your tears rain down upon your breast.
I have broken your heart with grief.

The Lady (*Soprano*)
You must not now, a new bridegroom,
Coldly leave your fair bride all alone,
Deserting her embrace for me.
If you do so, if you persist,
Disaster will befall your parents and yourself.

The Lover (*Male Falsetto*)
Cast aside your troubled looks
My lovely one,
And let us pass just one hour of this night,
Just once, no more,
In carefree union through the midnight hours.
Let me gather you again in my arms
With lasting joy
Time can never scatter or destroy.

Liu Pang's Legendary Rise to Power

LIU PANG'S LEGENDARY RISE TO POWER

(A Story from Shanghai)

L IU Pang[1], was born in the Prefecture of Ch'in, known nowaday
as P'enghsien in Kiangsu Province. He was born into
a poor family and never had any training for a trade or a
profession so, when he grew from a boy to a youth, the only
job he could get was that of a messenger boy for the local
magistrate.

As time went on he was promoted to be a police sergeant
whose duties were to trace down thieves and robbers. Although
Liu Pang was not well educated, he had a remarkable degree
of poise and self-assurance and was also very anxious to get on
in the world. In addition, he was inordinately fond of wine
and women. When he had no money to buy wine, he used to
go to the wine-shop and get his supplies on credit, then later on,
when he was in funds, he would pay the shopkeeper twice what
he owed. He used money like water and never behaved in the
least like a poor man who turned each penny over twice before
parting with it.

One day, he went on official business to Chung-An where
he happened to see the official procession of the first Emperor
of the Ch'in Dynasty. When he saw the splendour and
magnificence of the imperial procession he took a deep breath
and exclaimed, 'Why shouldn't an enterprising man attain even
to that height?'

---

1. The first emperor of the Han Dynasty.

Now it happened that Liu Kung, who was a native of Tan Fu and was also a close friend of the magistrate of P'enghsien, arrived in P'enghsien from Tan Fu to escape from his enemies. When the chief officials of P'enghsien learned that Liu Kung was the important guest of their magistrate they arranged to give a subscription reception and banquet in his honour, and Hsiao Ho, one of the P'enghsien officials was put in charge of collecting the subscriptions and arranging the grand reception at which Liu Kung was to be guest of honour.

When the men who had promised subscriptions were arriving for the banquet, Hsiao Ho announced, 'Those who are subscribing less than one thousand cash should sit at the lower end of the hall.'

Liu Pang, in the main, despised these minor officials of P'enghsien. On this occasion he followed in their wake as they entered the banqueting hall, for, although in fact he hadn't a penny to his name he had written down on his card of admission that he would subscribe ten thousand cash.

When Liu Kung saw what Liu Pang had written on his admission card, at first, he could hardly believe his eyes, and then, he hurried to the door to welcome him in.

Now Liu Kung was skilful at reading men's characters from their faces and, when he saw Liu Pang he was so impressed with what he read in his face of the true character of the man that he treated him with profound respect and led him to the seat of highest honour. As for Liu Pang, he accepted the honour done to him with the utmost composure.

When the banquet ended, Liu Kung detained Liu Pang and said to him, 'In my younger days, I studied the art of reading men's characters in their faces. I have studied many, many faces, but not one of them has interested me as much as yours does.

I hope that you will not neglect your opportunities nor waste your talents. I have a daughter. I will give her to you to be your wife, to look after you and your house and home.'

After Liu Pang had left, Liu Kung's wife reproached him, saying, 'You have always said that your daughter had very good prospects—that it was written so in her face—and that she would surely marry a man of official rank. Why then have you, in this casual way, promised her to this fellow Liu Pang?'

Liu Kung answered her, 'A decision of that kind is beyond the powers of any woman to understand.'

With these words, Liu Kung overcame his wife's objections and, in due course, Liu Pang married the girl.

*   *   *   *   *   *

Now the first Emperor of the Ch'in Dynasty was a great patron of architecture and, during his own lifetime, he built his own tomb at Li Shan in the Liu Tung district of Shensi Province.

This tomb was a very large-scale construction for which the emperor commanded every prefecture and district throughout the kingdom to provide conscript labourers and send them to Li Shan. So it came about that poor peasant farmers had to abandon their fields, their parents, their wives, their homes, in order to do forced labour for the emperor. P'enghsien was no exception. And so the magistrate, having to conscript a labour force, gathered together several hundred peasant farmers and gave Liu Pang the responsibility of escorting them to Li Shan.

Now, as we well know, Liu Pang was very fond of the bottle, and so, while en route, escorting the conscripts to Li Shan, he quite often got drunk. On several occasions while he was drunk, some of the labourers seized the chance to run away. In this way, he hadn't travelled far before at least half of his men had made off.

When Liu Pang saw this he thought to himself, 'At this rate, I shall have no men left by the time I reach Li Shan.'

Now the laws of the Ch'in Dynasty were very strictly enforced, and the penalty for desertion was death. So, when they got as far as Funghsien, Liu Pang ordered his gang of conscripts to halt. He then bought a generous supply of meat and wine and gave them a big feast. Then when night fell, he told them they were released from further service and added, 'You may go your several ways. From now on, I am an outlaw.'

When the conscripts heard this, they were all deeply grateful to him, but among them a dozen or more strong and fearless men declared their intention of following him into exile. So, Liu Pang and his band of about twelve strong and fearless men chose one of their number to be a scout and, under cover of darkness, to explore for them the narrow path which would lead them to their chosen place of exile.

The scout soon returned and reported, 'The path ahead is blocked by a huge snake!'

When Liu Pang, who was still under the influence of drink, heard this, he declared, 'When a strong and fearless man is on a journey, what can make him afraid!'

With these words he rushed ahead, drew out this sword and cut the snake in two. This done, he marched on for several more *li* until, overcome by the effects of alcohol, he dropped asleep by the roadside.

The story goes that near that place an old peasant woman stood by the roadside sobbing bitterly. A passing traveller stopped and asked her why she was weeping, and the old woman replied, 'Someone has murdered my son.'

The traveller then asked, 'Why was your son murdered? Who do you think could have done it?'

The old woman replied, 'My son was the son of the White King. He had changed himself into a white snake and lay blocking the road, and there he lies slain by the son of the Red King!'

The traveller was very frightened when he heard this story and wondered whether he had not enountered a ghost. With this thought in mind, he was just going to strike the old woman when she vanished away. At this, the traveller was even more frightened so he hastened on his way.

Now it so happened that, in his haste, he ran into Liu Pang who was just rousing himself from his drunken sleep, so he poured out his tale into Liu Pang's ears. When Liu Pang had listened to what the man had to say, his heart was so filled with pride and joy that he felt himself superior to any man alive.

From that time on, Liu Pang, because he did not dare to return home, established himself with his dozen or more fearless followers in the valley which lies between the Lin Huei and Li Shan mountain ranges. His wife often came to visit him there and, each time, she had no difficulty in discovering his hide-out. So Liu Pang asked her, 'How do you discover my hide-out so easily every time?'

His wife replied, 'There's always a cloud, like a nimbus, hovering above the place where you lie concealed. I only have to find my way to where the nimbus hovers, and then it's easy to find you.'

When Liu Pang heard his wife say this, his heart once more filled with pride and joy.

And from that time on, people throughout the P'enghsien district believed that Liu Pang was no ordinary mortal, and, a few at a time, they came to join his band of outlaws.

Now when the First Emperor of the Ch'in Dynasty died, the Second Emperor succeeded to the throne, but, because the common people could no longer bear the tyranny and oppressive laws of the Ch'in Dynasty, Ch'en Hsing and Wu Kuang seized the opportunity to raise the standard of revolt in Ch'ihsien. They cut down trees to make wooden cutlasses and swords, and they cut down bamboo to make poles to hold aloft their flags and banners. The people, who rallied to their call, killed the local district officials, occupied the cities and raised a militia to oppose the dynastic government.

The movement spread far and wide. Peace and order were overthrown throughout the land. Local roving gangs organized themselves and finally overthrew the Ch'in Dynasty and broke the line of succession.

This rebellion had its repercussions in P'enghsien. The common people there were naturally in ferment over the situation, for there were many rumours in circulation. The chief magistrate of P'enghsien was very afriad. So he decided he would voluntarily join the movement to overthrow the Ch'in Dynasty, and thus, he would ensure his own safety by raising the standard of revolt and joining forces with Ch'en Hsing.

At that time, Hsiao Ho was still an official at P'enghsien so he approached the chief magistrate and said, 'Sir, you are an appointed magistrate of the Ch'in Dynasty. If you now make a move to join forces with Ch'en Hsing the chances are the common people will not rally to your standard. Your best plan is to call upon those men, hundreds of them, who are in exile and appeal to them to return and defend P'enghsien. If you do this, the people of P'enghsien will not dare to disobey your orders.'

Acting on this advice the magistrate sent Fan Huei to command Liu Pang to return to P'enghsien.

Liu Pang who had already attracted several hundred men to join him, responded to the call and returned with Fan Huei to P'enghsien.

Now when the magistrate of P'enghsien saw that Liu Pang and his men were on their way back to the city he was afraid that a revolt had been planned. So he ordered the city gates to be closed and strong guards to be set. He also commanded that Liu Pang should be refused entry into the city and that Hsiao Ho should be put to death. But Hsiao Ho hurriedly fled from the city and joined himself to Liu Pang's followers. Then Liu Pang wrote a letter, affixed it to an arrow and shot it over the wall into the city. The letter which he addressed to the city elders, read as follows:

'The armies of the revolution have been victorious throughout the kingdom. At the command of your magistrate, you, the city elders are ready to defend P'enghsien. An army of the revolution has now arrived which will take your city and all the inhabitants will be put to the sword, so it is better for you to kill your magistrate and set up a strong leadership which reflects the spirit of the revolution. In this way you will deliver your homes, your families and yourselves from certain destruction.'

When the city elders read this missive they were all of one mind that the advice was sound. So they incited the people to murder their magistrate. Then they opened the city gates and welcomed Liu Pang to enter and be their governor.

Liu Pang again and again declined the offer, but as no one else dared to become leader of the revolutionary faction the people declared him to be their leader and acclaimed him Lord of P'enghsien.

The Dropped Fan

THE DROPPED FAN

WHAT is the story of the dropped fan? It begins with a young lady of the Sung Dynasty who was preparing to go for a walk in the Spring time to see the Festival of Spring and accidentally dropped from her balcony a fan upon which she had painted her own portrait. Now it so happened that a young squire of good family, who was also a scholar, saw it as he was passing by and picked it up. When he saw the portrait he fell head over heels in love with the young lady's likeness and desired above all things to lay his devotion at her feet. But at that time a wide gulf of etiquette separated the world of men from the world of women. Each world had its own code of behaviour so that it was impossible for young people to meet freely. So, after some time spent in fruitless enquiry, the young squire went to consult a friend. Together they made enquiries everywhere and eventually discovered that the young lady was the daughter of a military officer, a captain in the Imperial Army.

Now at the time of this story, the members of the captain's household were organizing a troupe of female actors. What is a troupe of female actors, you may ask? Well, in those days all actors were men; no rôles were taken by women. But this captain originated a new fashion by organizing a completely female troupe to perform operas.

At the time of this story every rôle in the opera they were rehearsing had been cast except that of a District Officer. Meanwhile, after racking his brains, this young scholar seized upon the idea of persuading a female go-between to make him up as a young woman and sell him into the captain's family as a household slave.

Now the head of the household, the young lady's father, was named Lu Ch'i and the daughter's name was Lu Hsing-yün, while the young squire, who was a very sentimental young fellow was named Chou Hsioh-wên.

Chou Hsioh-wên succeeded in impersonating a young woman and in being sold into the Lu household, but, such strict vigilance was kept over all comings and goings that for the whole of a month or six weeks he never caught even a glimpse of the young lady.

Now about this time a very good friend of Chou Hsioh-wên's Sen Chan-ch'ing, who was the holder of a Second Class Degree in the Imperial Examination, called at the Lu's house to see his friend and wanted urgently to talk with him because his father had come back from a pilgrimage to the temples at Soochow and Hangchow. But the meeting was difficult to arrange because Chou Hsioh-wên was impersonating a woman, while Sen Chan-ch'ing was a mere man. How could a young man and young woman contrive to have a tête à tête? That was Sen Chan-ch'ing's problem. Finally he had a bright idea, a real inspiration. He went to the Lu's house, from which you would hear the 'Ting-Bong, Ting-Bong' of small gongs coming from somewhere inside, and there he asked Lu Ch'i what was going on.

Lu Ch'i replied, 'That is the troupe of female actors I have organized. They're practising for a production.'

Sen Chan-ch'ing answered in a surprised tone, 'Indeed! that's something new. I've never seen female actors before. Would you let me take a look at them? Could you arrange for me to meet them as individuals?'

To this, Lu Ch'i replied, 'Certainly! certainly!'—and he sent word for the members of the cast to come out and meet the visitor.

Now Chou Hsioh-wên, who was the newly-added member of the cast, guessed that his friend had come to see him so he refused to show himself and hid himself inside the house. But Sen Chan-ch'ing was very wily and thought to himself, 'Ah, my good friend, it's no good hiding yourself! Your father has already returned from his pilgimage—is it right that on his return you should not be there to greet him? Fortunately for me, your servant knew what tricks you were up to when you left your house a month and more ago, and, knowing that you and I were close friends, came to confide in me. So I have no alternative but to come here to find you.'

Now Sen Chan-ch'ing was also an amateur actor and so, when he had met all the ladies of the cast, he said to Lu Ch'i, 'You have an excellent cast for your opera but you seem to be one member short. Now who could that be? Yes—I have it! You lack the person who plays the District Officer.'

After a moment's thought Lu Ch'i replied, 'Let me see—we do have someone cast for the rôle of the District Officer—and a very handsome young man she makes! She's highly educated and intelligent too. You don't have to teach that young person how to sing either—she has a natural aptitude for it. She only has to hear a tune once and she has the song by heart.'

As he said this the old man glowed with pleasure, 'Ah! she might even be a suitable match for you, young sir!'

'Enough of that, Old Gaffer,' was Sen Chan-ch'ing's reply to that suggestion. Yes, he even dared to address the master of the house as 'Old Gaffer'.

Lu Ch'i gave himself time to take in what the young man had said, thinking to himself, 'Never mind, as long as he doesn't call me some kind of whelp.' Then aloud he said, 'Yes. We have someone playing the District Officer.'

'Indeed! Where is she?' asked Sen Chan-ch'ing. 'It seems she's not here. What does she look like in the part? Can you arrange for me to see her too? Have you any more members of the troupe hiding away inside?'

Lu Ch'i looked around the cast. 'Let me see—now I come to think of it the lady who plays the District Officer is Suang Hsi. You're right; she hasn't come out. I'll send one of my servants to bring her here.'

Now most of the servants of Lu Ch'i household were sensible fellows, but the only one within calling distance at that moment was one who went by the nickname Snotty Nose, so Lu Ch'i was angry.

When Snotty Nose heard the master of the house calling for someone he stepped forward and asked, 'What do you want, master?'

'Why hasn't Suang Hsi come out?'

'Do you mean Suang Hsi who is playing the District Officer?'

'Yes. That's exactly what I do mean!'

'Master! Suang Hsi who plays the District Officer is looking very seedy. She's inside, holding both hands to her stomach and groaning, 'Ai-yah! Ai-yah! I've got a terrible stomach ache!'

'Oh—so that's why she hasn't come out with the rest; she's got a bad stomach ache.'

When Sen Chan-ch'ing heard this explanation he thought to himself, 'I see what your little game is, my friend. I can see what you're up to. You're trying to pull the wool over my eyes. What you really mean, my friend, is that you are not going to show yourself. I know all about that kind of stomach ache!'

Then he pondered afresh, 'It's a pity he refuses to come out. I've got to find some way of meeting him this very day before I leave this place. Besides, a man has his own self-respect to think of. If I let him get away with this I shall lower myself in my own esteem. Just think of it. I am now called Sen the Tiger, although I have never actually devoured anyone, but if I don't see this thing through, folks will call me Sen the Chicken Hearted.

'Let me see. I have come here today and have succeeded in seeing nine of the cast, but the tenth, their star actress, is hiding inside the house. I happen to have a very dogged temperament. If I had failed entirely to see any of the troupe I would have called it a day, but I've succeeded in seeing nine of them. It's *that* that gives *me* the stomach ache! Ai-yah! truly it gives me the gripes! To think that he should try to make a fool of me!'

Meanwhile Lu Ch'i was thinking to himself, 'What kind of fellow is this? He has met nine out of the ten members of my troupe and now he complains that he can't meet the tenth member—and she suffering from stomach ache too!'

Then as Lu Ch'i was a military man he turned his wrath upon Snotty Nose (whose real name was Lu Fu) who promptly answered his stern look with, 'Yes, master?'

'Go inside and fetch Suang Hsi here.'

'Yes master!—but Suang Hsi's got the stomach ache!'

'Stomach ache or no stomach ache, go and fetch her here!'

'Yes sir!' But even while Snotty Nose was making this answer he was grumbling under his breath, 'There's nothing I can do about it. My master gives an order and I have to obey. This will surely end the argument. I have no choice in the matter; so in I go to fetch Suang Hsi.'

Meanwhile the so-called Suang Hsi was waiting inside for the word that would release her from her predicament.

Now you may be wondering how Chou Hsioh-wên, who was about six feet tall, could have managed to impersonate a young woman and to speak with the refined voice of a young lady. Be your answer what you will, Snotty Nose now began to be rather fresh with Chou Hsioh-wên thinking that the District Officer of the play was in reality a woman. Although Chou Hsioh-wên addressed the servant correctly as 'Brother' and the servant addressed him as 'Sister', Chou Hsioh-wên was thinking to himself, all the time, 'What is this rogue of a servant really up to? A man who sets himself to flirt with a young lady is well aware that he is flirting with a member of the tender sex and this fellow comes and addresses me as if I am indeed a young woman. I wonder what his game is?' Then he turned to Snotty Nose. 'Brother—'

'Yes, sister?'

'Has the young man Sen who was waiting outside gone away yet?'

'No. He pointed to the actor list hanging outside there and demanded to see you personally. What makes you think he has gone away?'

'Ai-yah! What shall I do!' And then Suang Hsi added in a deeply anxious tone, 'Why did he insist upon my going out to meet him?'

'Your guess is as good as mine,' replied Snotty Nose.

'Mm-mm' pondered Suang Hsi half aloud, 'I'm scared to death that this fellow knows something about me.'

Then he said aloud, 'What on earth brings this Sen fellow here now?' Then he chanted.

> *'I parted from my friend a month ago,*
> *I said farewell to him a month ago.'*

But behind this ditty Chou Hsioh-wên was hiding his real anxiety. 'My friend and I,' he was thinking 'have been in the habit of spending every evening together and some part at least of every day as well. It's now a month and more since we saw one another. It's natural that he is missing me. Besides, he knows that I came here about six weeks ago and he probably thinks I have surely seen the young lady of the fan by now. He doubtless fondly imagines we are already on familiar terms, already whispering sweet nothings to one another. You little know, my good friend, that so far I've not had even one glimpse of the young lady! You know I became a member of the women's quarters of this household so that I could find the lady of the fan, but you don't know, by a long stretch, that I'm still ten thousand miles from even setting my eyes on her. As for your demand to see me, if I go out now to meet you, I as a servant, will have to kow-tow to you before I address you!—I, kow-tow to Sen Chan-ch'ing!!—Not that an isolated kow-tow has any particular significance but you will hold it over me next time we meet. It looks very much as if I shall have to give this sentimental friend of mine the advantage over me this time, otherwise Papa Lu will have grounds to suspect something. There's no help for it. I'll just have to go out and face him. I can't go on hiding here indefinitely; that much is clear. Once the cat is out of the bag, I shan't know where to turn. So here goes! I just have to go out and meet the pestilent fellow!'

Then he turned to the servant. 'Brother,' he said, 'if that man outside has truly asked by name to see me, help me to go out and meet him.'

'Trust me, sister, as you would your own brother.' And with these words Snotty Nose led the way to the door.

'Yes; I'm with you—I'm following you,' said Chou Hsioh-wên.

'Listen, sister,' whispered the servant. Then he stopped short.

'Yes, brother.'

'Er—haven't you just been having a bad stomach ache?'

'Yes; that's so.'

'After such severe stomach pains you're probably not yet very steady on your feet.'

'I think I can manage.'

'Suppose you steady yourself by putting your honourable hand on my unworthy shoulder.'

'Ah! That's better!' But even as Chou Hsioh-wên accepted the offer he thought to himself, 'The language this fellow uses when he asks me to put my hand on his shoulder is the language of an inferior to a superior; it is not the language used between fellow-servants. He speaks of my "honourable hand" and talks of my placing it upon his "unworthy shoulder". I know what I'll do. I'll lean my whole weight upon his shoulder so that he will have some inkling that I'm a man and won't be guessing so completely in the dark. All the same, seeing he doesn't know my secret, I can't blame him for trying to flirt with me. . .' Then he said to Snotty Nose, 'Brother, I'm sorry if I have offended you.' And with these words he clamped his hand down like a vice upon Snotty Nose's shoulder.

'Ouch!' When the weight of that hand descended upon his shoulder Snotty Nose felt as if a thunderbolt had struck him. 'Ouch, sister!!' he exclaimed. 'Go easy!'

'Ha-ha!!' laughed Chou Hsioh-wên to himself.

Now that rascally rogue of a servant was so taken by surprise that he trembled from head to foot. But when he looked at Chou Hsioh-wên's hand resting on his shoulder he saw that it was as white as driven snow and soft as thistledown. He felt that it was so deliciously tender that a man might be forgiven if he felt tempted to dip it in soya sauce and gobble it up.

The more Snotty Nose gazed upon that tender hand the more he wished to take it in his own, but he was afraid 'Little Sister' would box his ears if he went too far. So he was in a fix over what he would do about it. All he could do was to turn his head and gaze devotedly upon Chou Hsioh-wên's hand and stroke it with his chin.

Now would you believe it—that rascal of a servant hadn't shaved for several days; so his beard and whiskers were as hard and stiff as the bristles of a broom. All unconcious of this, he rubbed his chin upon the back of Chou Hsioh-wên's hand, nurmuring as he did so, 'Ah! sister! Ah, sister! ah!—a-ah!—a-a-ah!! I've got a chance to caress the back of your tender hand!'

Chou Hsioh-wên thought to himself, 'You rascally puppy! You caress the back of my hand with your chin and it feels as painful to me as if you were stroking it with the bristles of a broom. If you think you are going to play a practical joke on me, that's fine. I'm your match at that game.' And he clamped down his hand even more heavily on Snotty Nose's shoulder, chanting as he did so,

Ah—a-ah—a-a-ah!
A soft hand on your shoulder,
Oh so gentle, oh so light;
A lover's touch so tender
Speaks in signs, not words.

While softly chanting this ditty he gave Snotty Nose's shoulder muscles a twist, thinking as he did so, 'If this fellow wants to play tricks on me, I'll give him as good as I get. Suppose I give him another hint that I'm a man.' And so he shook

Snotty Nose by the shoulder chanting as he did so,

> *'I'll shake, I'll shake*
> *The greengage tree,*
> *The unripe plums will fall.'*

At this Snotty Nose laughed outright and jumped for joy. His whole body seemed to melt in ectasy, his mouth watered with anticipated joys till the saliva dripped from his mouth. Beside himself with happiness, he beamed at Chou Hsioh-wên murmuring, 'Ah sister! Ah, sister, mine!'

'Yes, brother?'

'Sister—, er—sister, er—don't forget you are wanted outside.'

'I haven't forgotten.'

'Ah sister! Ah sister mine! When you go outside you must remember to keep a very straight face when you answer any question.'

'What will happen if I laugh, brother?'

'Ooh, sister! Ooh! you know how to behave better than that. If you laugh only once, you'll risk losing your job with the Old Man—then all will be at an end between us; goodbye for ever to any thought of marriage.'

'Listen brother. Any thought of marriage between you and me is entirely out of the question. You are in danger of making a big mistake: a marriage between us is right out of the question.

> *Tra-la-lala-lala la!*
> *A man betrothed to a man, aha!*
> *No wedding can take place, aha!'*

'What are you saying, addressing me as your brother?'

'You can guess the answer for yourself.'

'Sister mine, sister dear,' pleaded Snotty Nose,

'A big chopper is waiting, my dear,
To chop off our romance, I fear.'

'You call my visitor a chopper? Tell me, what do you really think of my friend, this man who calls himself Sen?'

'He has taken Second Class honours in the Imperial Examinations, but he takes First Class Honours with the ladies.'

'You say my friend is over-fond of the ladies! Nothing is further from the truth. His first love is the flowing cup. Given that, he has no time for the fair sex. But as for you—that's a different story. Look out for trouble, you rogue for making sheep's eyes at me, a man!'

'I understand your pretty game! Just wait awhile, and we shall see. But for now, follow me and we'll meet this fellow who is waiting for you outside.'

'I'll follow where you lead.' And with these words Snotty Nose and Chou Hsioh-wên started once more to go out. But just as they were approaching the screen that blocks the view of outsiders looking in through the big doors, Chou Hsioh-wên withdrew his hand from Snotty Nose's shoulder.

'Sister!!' pleaded Snotty Nose, 'keep your hand there; no one will read anything into it. Even if our master sees you with your hand on my shoulder, he won't say antying. Remember, you've got a bad stomach ache. You need to lean on me for support.'

But Chou Hsioh-wên thought to himself, 'Brother, if you don't look out you're going to trip over the raised doorsill. Your mind is on my hand resting on your shoulder; you have no eyes for that door-sill in front of your nose. Tripping over the door-sill will teach you a nice lesson.'

With this thought, Chou Hsion-wên raised his hand ready to thump it with all his force on Snotty Nose's shoulder thinking to himself, 'I've somehow got to get it into this fellow's head that I am a man, and that I'm a man of military training at that.' Then, putting his thoughts into deeds he once more thumped his hand down heavily onto Snotty Nose's shoulder.

Now even without a push Snotty Nose would have tripped over the raised door-sill, but with the heavy push Chou Hsioh-wên gave him, he fell sprawling sooner and more heavily than he would have done without that help.

'So sorry,' murmured Chou Hsioh-wên. But even though he apologized, the force with which his hand had fallen upon Snotty Nose's shoulder was like that which farm labourers use when with all their might and with accurate aim they hurl up bundles of hay onto a haystack. As a result, Snotty Nose tripped and fell heavily over the door-sill crying out loudly as he fell, 'Ooh! Ooh!' He cried out so loud that his master called out, 'What do you think you're doing in there, you stupid, clumsy fellow?'

'Master!' replied Snotty Nose. But instead of finishing the sentence, he went on speaking aloud to himself, 'What a clumsy fool you are. You don't even know how to take a fall properly!'

'What do you mean, you idiot?' said his master. 'What do you mean by saying that I don't even know how to fall down properly!'

By this time Snotty Nose had scrambled to his feet. The fall had made him giddy and his face was suffused scarlet as he pulled himself together and announced formally, 'Enter Suang Hsi!!'

'You pig-headed fool!' replied his master.

'Yes, sir!' replied Snotty Nose. Then he stood on one side muttering to himself, 'Ai-yah!—I could kill myself, making a mistake like that. It's one thing to announce the entry of the master of the house like that, but I must have been crazy to have announced a fellow servant in that way.'

While Snotty Nose was sighing over his blunder, Chou Hsioh-wên tripped daintly forward and bowed low to his master saying as he did so, 'Suang Hsi pays humble respects to her master.'

'It's very nice to hear courteous words correctly spoken like that!' muttered Snotty Nose, still trying to collect his scattered wits.

'That will do, Suang Hsi,' said the master.

'Thank you, master. What is your wish?'

'Master Sen is here asking to meet you. Go over and pay your respects to him.'

'Yes master, I will do as you say.'

Then Chou Hsioh-wên cast his eyes around the group thinking to himself, 'Look at my good friend standing over there, so serious, so straight faced that even a mouse couldn't find a crease to use as a foothold to climb up by. He stands so pokerfaced that a kick on the shins couldn't make him wrinkle his expression. That's the straight face that's waiting to hear me call him "Master Sen," is it! Very well, I've consented to come out here this morning to see you, my friend, but how am I going to avoid having to kow-tow to you and address you subserviently as "Master Sen"? I honestly cannot bring myself to do that. The thing to do is to play for time and then see how matters work out.'

With this resolution Chou Hsioh-wên walked over to his friend thinking to himself, 'If I don't address him as "Master Sen", what on earth can I call him? I know—I'll pretend that I've forgotten his name—that I have difficulty in recalling it.'

'Er-er,' he began.

Sen Chan-ch'ing heard this 'E—er', and thought, 'That's strange. He stutters 'Er-er' and is at a loss for a single word to follow on with.'

Chou Hsioh-wên began again, 'Er—This—er—, That—er—, Mr. What's your name—er—'

'What's that you're saying?'

'I beg your pardon.'

Sen Chan-ch'ing was thinking, 'Aha, my good man, you haven't yet addressed me as "Master Sen" and I am resolved to make you do it. I don't let you get away without addressing me in that honorific way. I'm, just going to dig my heels in until you do so.'

Then he put on a very severe countenance and said, 'My dear woman, I think I know who you are.'

When Chou Hsioh-wên heard these words he thought to himself, 'Be careful, my friend, this isn't the time for you to say you know me.' Then he added aloud, 'I swear you don't know me!' still avoiding addressing him by his name and the proper respectful prefix.

'What do you mean by saying that I don't know you. Your surname is Chou.'

'If he utters one word more,' thought Chou Hsioh-wên to himself, 'the game will be up! If he adds my name "Hsioh-wên" what then will become of me! What on earth shall I do! I haven't a moment to lose in case he spills the whole story.' Then he said aloud, 'Master Sen, your obedient servant is not surnamed Chou.'

At this Sen Chan-ch'ing laughed outright, 'Ha-ha-ha!' while thinking to himself, 'I'm not going to let you get away with that! I'm going to make you address me properly as

"Master Sen" before I let you off.' But aloud he said, 'Yes-yes. I must be mistaken; my memory must have played me false. You are the daughter of the Chou family's neighbour, aren't you?'

'Yes, I am.'

'Ah, that's why your face is so very familiar to me.'

At this Chou Hsioh-wên thought to himself 'You have given me a big fright, my friend. At your mention of the surname "Chou" great beads of sweat have broken out all over me.'

Then Sen Chan-ch'ing continued, 'You live in the same village as the Chou's, don't you?'

'Yes, I do.'

'—and your surname is Hu, and your father is Hu Li, isn't he? And your full name is Hu T'u[1].'

'Yes, it is,' replied Chou. But within himself he was thinking, 'My good friend, you're making this story up as you go along. You know more about me than I know myself!'

'Of course I know you,' continued Sen. 'Your father was a farm-labourer on my father's farm, and you often used to come to our house. At that time you had two little pigtails and a runny nose. Isn't that so? Or maybe you have forgotten those days.'

'I well remember them.'

'I gather from your master that he has bought you as a household slave and that you are now cast for the rôle of the District Officer in his troupe of female actors. Is that so?'

'Yes.'

'How long have you been here?'

---

1. The two names combined are a pun in Shanghai dialect upon Hu Li Hu t'u (胡裏胡塗) meaning 'stupid'.

'I was sold into service here on the fourth day of the third month.'

'Oh—then you have been here a month and more by now. Your master tells me that you have proved to be a very fine and intelligent actress.'

'Far otherwise.'

'Your master tells me he's very pleased with your acting.'

'Far otherwise! As a matter of fact the rôle of the District Officer is a very difficult part to play.'

'I have a question to ask you. Do you know the play called Ten Thousand Dollars? Are you acquainted with it?[2]'

'I see your little game, my friend,' thought Chou Hsioh-wên. 'You're fishing to know whether I've yet met the daughter of the house.'

Now how did Chou Hsioh-wên guess that Sen was referring to his secret plan to meet the lady of the fan? He did so from the stilted way in which his friend had said, 'Do you know the play Ten Thousand Dollars—are you acquainted with it?' in which the term 'Ten Thousand Dollars' is a poetic way of saying 'The Daughter—have you met her?'

'My good friend,' thought Chou to himself, 'you little realize that I've not met her yet.' But aloud he said, 'I'm not yet acquainted with the 'Ten Thousand Dollars' you speak of.'

'You haven't yet come across it?'

'No, not yet.'

'That's not very enterprising of you. You will have to do better than that if you are to live up to the expectations of your master. You should be a little more venturesome. The title rôle is a very difficult one to act.'

'Is it?'

---

2. In Chinese the pronoun t'a (他) denotes either him, her or it. In English the ambiguity is lost.

Overhearing this, Lu Ch'i muttered to himself, 'What does this fellow mean? advising Suang Hsi about her role, as if she did not know it very well indeed already. Maybe her diffident replies are due to her modesty about her real skills as an actress.' So you can see Lu Ch'i was still completely in the dark about the romantic intrigue going on under his own nose.

'Now I have something else to tell you,' Sen Chan-ch'ing went on.

'Yes, what is it?'

'Your father came to our place and told me that he had sold you into this household. He was so overjoyed to get the money they gave for you that he went off on a pilgrimage to some temples to burn incense there. Now he has come back again from his pilgrimage. So he has asked me to think out a way of getting you back again for him. He thinks of you constantly.'

'So that's why you've come here—because my father has returned from his journey. Now I understand why you wanted to see me.'

'Can you let him know when you are likely to finish learning your part?'

'It will probably take me a few more days from now.'

'If you work very hard at it, about how many days? Can you give me any idea?'

'I think I can manage it by the fifteenth of the fifth month— the time of the Dragon Boat Festival.'

'That's only a few days from now. Do your best to be perfect in the part by then. You must live up to the expectations which others have of you.'

'I understand.'

'You may go now, madam.'

'Goodbye.'

'I hope we shall meet again.' And with these words Sen Chan-ch'ing let Chou Hsioh-wên go off to one side. Then he turned to Lu Ch'i and said, 'This little District Officer is really very good—so very good-looking and with such a clear speaking voice. She's truly very good. You'd hardly credit that she's only a household slave from one of the villages. I must go now.'

Then Lu Ch'i gave orders for the people in the kitchen to prepare a meal and set it on with some simple wine.

'You're taking far too much trouble. I've already troubled you far too much, I don't want to trouble you any more by staying to dinner. I truly mean it—I do indeed.'

'Don't stand on ceremony. As the saying goes, anyone who comes here is always as welcome as if he were in his own home. That holds for you.'

'Next time I come to see you, you won't feel you're in my debt! Sorry; I have to go now.'

'Then at least let me see you off.'

'You don't have to take all that trouble.'

Then, with many exchanges of bows and courtesies they made their way to the outer door where Sen Chan-ch'ing got into his waiting sedan chair, and returned home followed by his footmen.

When Sen reached home the bearers stopped and he descended from his chair. Then he entered his own home. When he had sat down in the guest-hall, he called a servant and told him to go to Chou Hsioh-wên's house and tell Chou's father that he had a message for him to say that Chou Hsioh-wên would be away from home for a few days and that he wouldn't be back until the Dragon Boat Festival.

We will now leave Sen Chan-ch'ing for the time being and return to the Lu household.

When Lu Ch'i had seen Sen Chan-ch'ing off he returned to the inner room, walking backwards in the courteous manner appropriate for seeing off an honoured guest, while Snotty Nose closed the outer door firmly and then set to work tidying up here and there. As for the young ladies they went off to the room where they had been rehearsing. There they settled again down to rehearsing diligently, all except Chou Hsioh-wên. As for him, he was too heavy-hearted and worried to do any rehearsing that day.

You may ask why this was so.

Let me tell you. Chou Hsioh-wên knew that his old father was a very stern and quick-tempered man so when he learned that his father was back home again he knew that if his father found out that he was impersonating a young woman he would have to face his father's anger as well as the great displeasure of the family. So naturally he was very worried. He was frowning so much with anxiety that Mr. Chang Chun-wên, the director of the rehearsal, seeing his worried look spoke to him, 'Suang Hsi!'

'Yes, master?'

'You're looking worried and you're frowning badly. What's worrying you?'

'I've had bad news. My father has come home and I'm worried because I'm not there to greet him. I'm not able to tell you the whole story.'

Then he said to himself, 'What shall I do? A few minutes ago, I was pretending that I had the stomach ache; but I've now got a real stomach ache—the kind of stomach ache that no one else can either realize or do anything about.' But aloud he said, 'Please, Sir, I've still got the stomach ache.'

'You've still got a pain in your stomach?'

'Yes, Sir.'

'Most likely you've caught a cold.   If I give you a half-holiday you can have a good rest.   Off you go; and mind you avoid eating anything cold.   Then come a little earlier tomorrow to do your rehearsing.'

'Thank you, Sir.'   And with these words Chou Hsioh-wên put away his copy of the play into the drawer and went out from the rehearsal room looking back cautiously over his shoulder as he made his way out.

'So far so good,' he thought to himself.   'That was a good idea, to pretend that I still had the stomach ache.

Lucky stomach ache, hurray!
Very sharp, sharp pain;
Lucky half-day holiday
I'll try that trick again.

I've escaped from that nuisance of a rehearsal, but how to find that lady's chamber I haven't the ghost of an idea:

From irksome dull lessons
I've now run away;
Now off to that lady's room,
But who knows the way?

There's no one will tell me
The way to her chamber,
So off to my own room
Full sadly I'll wander.

Tiptoe away, I go full soon
Away to the Plum Blossom Orchard Room
The little room where I sit and dream
Of the fairest face that ever I've seen.'

Then, not knowing what to do about finding the lady of his heart he went off to his sleeping quarters. When he got there he sat down facing the window lost in sad thought. 'The news my friend brought me just now means a bad look-out for me. He cleverly managed to let me know secretly that my father is home again from his pilgrimage to the temples in Soochow and Hangchow, and he tried very hard to worm out from me information about my success here. My family follows the old-fashioned ways very strictly. If I go home now the whole family will surely reprimand me severely and my father will certainly give me a beating. I'm scared! The best thing I can do is to remain here disguised as a maid-servant and to go on with the rehearsals of my part in the play.'

APPENDIX

The following notes on each story give information about the dialect, the type of story, the style in which it was told, and suggestions of analogous stories in other traditions.

1. **The Cock:** a folk tale of the 'just so' story kind, which includes the 'jewels' of a god's sententious advice to a wicked younger brother.

   Dialect: Shanghainese

   Narrative Style: *p'ing hua*

   Analogues: Kipling's *Just So Stories* (English)

2. **The Blockhead:** a moral story of the *exemplum* kind which points the stupidity of blindly memorized answers.

   Dialect: Cantonese

   Narrative Style: *p'ing hua*

   Analogues: *The Adventures of Little Black Sambo* (American)

3. **The Magic Treasure Pot:** a fairy tale which carries an implicit moral. The setting is realistic peasant life; the happenings are due to the magical intervention of a *hsien* to aid a poor family; but the magical power or object is withdrawn when an unworthy person seizes it and uses it for selfish ends.

Dialect: Hoi San (Kwangtung)

Narrative Style: *p'ing hua*

Analogues: *Sweet Porridge* (Scandinavian)
              The Fisherman and His Wife (German)
              The Wishing Table (Danish)

4. ***Fan Kiang-shan and the Tiger***: a folk tale of the 'just
   so' story type which is also a universal type of story of
   the poor boy who is able to outwit an enemy who has
   superior ferocity and strength.

Dialect: Mandarin

Narrative Style: *p'ing hua*

Source or District of Origin: Hunan

Analogues: *The Three Little Pigs* (English)
              The Valiant Little Tailor (German)

5. ***The Hair Rope Bridge***:   a legend which explains a natural
   phenomenon the real causes of which probably lie in
   remote folk memory.   Also a *hsien* story of the days when
   the daughters of heaven took husbands of the sons of men
   (cf. *Genesis* 6: 2).

Dialect: Cantonese

Narrative Style: *p'ing hua*

Source or District of Origin: probably Shensi or the West China Border.

Analogues: *The Book of Genesis*—the stories of *The Flood, The Tower of Babel, Lot's Wife* (Hebrew)

The Odyssey—Odysseus sails between Scylla and Charybdis (Greek)

The Legend of Giant's Causeway (Irish)

The Legend of Lorelei (German)

6. ***The Snake will Swallow the Elephant:*** a typical Chinese exemplary tale in explanation of a proverb. The pun contained in the title is a point of wit much appreciated by Chinese people in all walks of life.

Dialect: Cantonese

Narrative Style: *p'ing hua*

Analogues: *What the Good Man Does is Always Right* (Danish)

The Frog Prince (German)

Beauty and the Beast (English)

7. ***The Drum that Shook Heaven:*** a fairy (*hsien*) tale which centers on the universal folklore theme of the reciprocal love between an honest peasant and a captive princess who is unattainable until, by courage, ingenuity, and the magical aid of good fairies, the youth overcomes all obstacles to win her.

Dialect: Shanghainese

Narrative Style: *p'ing hua*

Source or District of Origin: The mountain temple with its monkey guardians may place the story in *Monkey Cave Temple* which is situated on a mountain peak in the Mount Omei area of South-West Szechuan. The millet places it definitely in North China.

Analogues: A combination of

> *Jack and the Beanstalk* (English) and
>
> *Rapunzel* (German).

8. *The Fish - Ended Roof Beam:* a *hsien* story several of which contain the deeds of *Lu Pan* the master carpenter who became a *hsien* and the 'patron saint' of all carpenters.

Dialect: Mandarin

Narrative Style: *p'ing hua*

Source or District of Origin: unidentified

Analogues: *The Bronze Boar* (Italian: retold by Hans Andersen)

9. *The Beggar Defeats the Professional Boxer:* a *hsien* story of the *wu hsia* type.

Dialect: Chao Chow (Kwangtung)

Narrative Style: p'ing hua

Source or District of Origin: Chengtu, Szechuan

Analogues: *Tales of Robin Hood* (English)

10. **Ho Wai-kwan's Vigil:** a romantic ballad of a forsaken mistress.

Dialect: Cantonese

Narrative Style: t'an-tz'ŭ to a *yang-ch'in* accompaniment.

Source or District of Origin: Canton, judging from the places named in the ballad.

11. **The Lover to his Former Mistress:** a romantic ballad of a dialogue between a forsaken mistress and the lover who has been forced into a marriage befitting his scholarship.

Dialect: Cantonese

Narrative Style: t'an-tz'ŭ to a *yang-ch'in* accompaniment.

Source or District of Origin: Canton

12. **Liu Pang's Rise to Power:** a popularized version of well-known chronicle history, in which myth, legend, and history are mingled.

Dialect: Cantonese

Narrative Style: p'ing hua

Source or District of Origin: *The Book of History* (史記) by Ssū-ma Chien (circ. 147-74 B.C.) An early chapter records the establishment of the Han Dynasty by Kao Chu following his killing of a white snake and contains, in brief, all the materials used by the story-teller.

13. *The Dropped Fan:* a romantic tale of a young man's witty escapade, disguised as a household slave, to gain sight of the inaccessible lady to whom he has sworn devotion through seeing her portrait.

Dialect: Soochow

Narrative Style: *t'an-tz'ŭ* with *san hsüen* accompaniment.

Source or District of Origin: Soochow (with the improvised parts original). The basic story is probably a traditional romance or an episode of such a romance.